THE DIPLOMATIST

By the same author

SLOW BURNER
THE TELEMANN TOUCH
VENETIAN BLIND
CLOSED CIRCUIT
THE ARENA
THE UNQUIET SLEEP
THE HIGH WIRE
THE ANTAGONISTS
THE HARD SELL
THE POWDER BARREL
THE POWER HOUSE
THE CONSPIRATORS
A COOL DAY FOR KILLING
THE DOUBTFUL DISCIPLE
THE HARDLINERS
THE BITTER HARVEST
THE PROTECTORS
THE LITTLE RUG BOOK (non-fiction)
THE OLD MASTERS
THE KINSMEN
THE SCORPION'S TAIL
YESTERDAY'S ENEMY
THE POISON PEOPLE
VISA TO LIMBO
THE MEDIAN LINE
THE MONEY MEN
THE MISCHIEF-MAKERS
THE HEIRLOOM
THE NEED TO KNOW
THE MARTELLO TOWER

THE DIPLOMATIST

William Haggard

Hodder & Stoughton
LONDON SYDNEY AUCKLAND TORONTO

C.2
S

British Library Cataloguing in Publication Data
Haggard, William
    The diplomatist.
    Rn. Richard Henry Michael Clayton
    I. Title
    823'.914[F]   PR6053.L38

    ISBN 0 340 41845 1

For
my favourite daughter-in-law

1

Clement Saint John, Prime Minister of the United Kingdom, was walking down Whitehall with an armed detective a pace behind him. He pronounced his name as it was written, Saint John, considering Sinjun an affectation. His background and his personal preference were both against affectation of any kind. The son of a country parsonage, the vicarage bread and butter was in his blood. His parents had taught him the lesson dourly: he was as good as the boys at the big house at Wykeham – better since they suspected them of all kinds of childish sin – but the difference was that he'd have to prove it. For these elegant Etonians had money and he had not. He would be given the best education which a Church of England parson could afford and thereafter he must fend for himself. Clement Saint John had understood perfectly. That meant service in some Colonial Police Force (in his boyhood they had still existed) or being articled to a local solicitor. Assuming he didn't wish to take Orders, a matter upon which his father had been scrupulously neutral. He had always been a scrupulous man.

So Clement Saint John walked down Whitehall reflectively. In an age of steadily swelling terrorism the Prime Minister had a bullet-proof car and Saint John had been pressed to use it more often. But he badly needed exercise, and though he resented the fact it was necessary he would accept that an armed man must march behind him. Blind terrorism was a fact and increasing. As it happened he was walking to the Security Executive of which he was, in a crisis, the Chairman, and which guarded the never defined arcana of threats to the State with a capital S.

But at this moment he wasn't thinking of terrorism nor of danger to the Prime Minister's person; he was wondering how he had reached that office when he'd never even considered doing so. Sara, he decided, his wife.

He also wondered how he had come to marry her since Sara was upper class and he was not. Such a difference didn't prohibit marriage but it made it in most ways very improbable. For one thing they were unlikely to meet, this granddaughter of the local potentate and a junior partner – he had reached that by now – in a firm of solicitors in the county town. But her father had used Saint John's senior partner and one day she had walked in with him and there it was.

He permitted a smile for she'd swept him off his feet. He had in fact had reservations for his upbringing had sounded a warning. The upper class had been faintly suspect, not because they were richer than you were (there was something in the Catechism about the station to which the Almighty had called you) but because in a pinch they would let you down, drop you dead and revert to their own unashamedly. But he'd been flattered and she'd been extremely attractive.

In the end he had proposed but still doubtfully for he had heard the gossip and gave it credence. His parents, if they'd still been alive, would have said that a girl like Sara had had a past. Nowadays one said 'had been around'. He had found that she certainly had and she'd scared him.

Now the smile was a grin for he hadn't objected. Nor to the later knowledge that she still travelled. For Sara had a Latin talent for pleasing two men at one time and doing it well. No nonsense about a dressing room because Sara had taken a lover on the side. The Prime Minister remembered an Italian proverb. If your wife was particularly sweet to you it was time to look under the bed for the other man.

And at this moment she was being particularly sweet again.

He shrugged for he was a disciplined realist. The world had changed since his own calm boyhood. He would have preferred a wife who was wholly faithful but Sara was always superbly discreet and he couldn't pretend that he minded that much. Pretending – to yourself or publicly – pretending was the ultimate sin.

And he wouldn't be where he was without her. He hadn't been a political animal and Sara notably had been and still was. She had made him stand for the County Council where he'd served with the cool efficiency which his father had shown on his pastoral round. And then there had been that by-election.

The Prime Minister smiled a second time. There were still a few constituencies like his, almost Rotten Boroughs, seats out of an updated Trollope. The patronage of two great local families wouldn't quite guarantee election but if they threw their weight against you the odds were short that you wouldn't get in. But in this case all the stops were pulled out for him. He had held the seat with a bigger majority and in the House he had been a hard-working backbencher till the Great Election had changed all that.

His train of thought was interrupted by a sense that the man behind him had checked. He turned and stared in silent astonishment: the guard was rigid, alert and balanced, and his hand had moved up to his armpit under his coat. He was looking at a bus which had moved away. A young Sikh in a *pakta* had just got down from it; he didn't even glance at Saint John but went off upon his business quietly.

The guard dropped his hand to his side as he disappeared, saying on a note of apology: "A Sikh, you know. We've been warned to be careful."

"I could see he was a Sikh myself. But he was only a boy."

"Boys can shoot too."

"Oh to hell," the Prime Minister said; he was annoyed. He accepted the disagreeable fact that he couldn't walk in a public street unguarded, but almost drawing a gun on a boy of twelve struck him as an over-reaction. "Come up beside me," he said. "I want to talk." The incident had absurdly upset him and a talk would relieve the tension which he despised. The guard came up level with him, and they walked on.

"What do you know about Sikhs, then?"

"I've been told they could give us trouble."

"They are. But not the sort of trouble you mean. Like everyone else they're split into parties: the ones content to stay in the Punjab and the others who want a state of their own. And I cannot say I in any way blame them. But several of the extremists are here and it's no secret the Indians want me to send them back. I haven't the least intention of doing so. It doesn't make for better relations and there's a powerful Indian lobby which I detest. I can't think why we keep the Commonwealth. It's a sham and I dislike pretences. It's more important to the Crown than to you or me. Not to put too fine a point on it the Palace has got the Commonwealth up its nose."

The guard had been interested but now was offended. He was a dyed-in-the-wool old-fashioned royalist and such talk he considered disrespectful. He began to slip back to his place a step behind.

The Prime Minister said without turning his head: "Why do you do that? I was talking."

And enjoying it, he thought but did not say. It was good to take the wraps off occasionally. Katharsis. A salubrious discharge of the emotions.

The guard said with a touch of surliness: "It's the way I've been taught to do it, sir."

"A better field of fire, you mean?"

10

"Something like that."

"Oh, very well."

Clement Saint John returned to reflection. So in the House he'd been a conscientious backbencher. Or had been until that astonishing election.

Which Sara had done so much to give him.

He hadn't been an impressive orator, certainly not in the windy Welsh manner, but he was a crisp and entirely lucid speaker. In such courts as he, a mere solicitor, was grudgingly allowed to appear he was effective for his varied clients and listened to with respect by the Bench. He gave the facts and gave them shortly, and on the political platform he did the same.

Sara had seen the potential at once for she came from a great political family. Once it had been firmly Whig and was still contemptuous of the Tory ethos. So why not stand up and tell the truth? People were sick and tired of the half of it, suspicious of pie in the sky for ever, more than suspicious of foolish optimism when they sensed that it was wholly unjustified. Such a course might lose him a vote or two but his own seat was pretty safe by now and there was a thinnish chance, no more than that, that a little of what he said might be noticed outside.

. . . Unemployment, then. An undoubted sore but it couldn't be dealt with sensibly as one evil. It was futile to talk of full employment. That would never exist and never had. What had existed had been overmanning, three men doing the work of two, for the Unions in the days of their arrogance had blackmailed employers, especially State industries, into manning levels which were wildly unjustified. Industry as a whole was healthier for a necessary but painful shake-out. At least a million unemployed had never had a real job at all.

There had been a mutter from the audience which had been fed on pap from its childhood and was surprised. A single voice called: "Well said," and that was all.

11

And worse than the evil of overmanning was the way that jobs had been graded upwards. In a car assembly plant he'd seen lately a wheel complete with tyre come down a chute. At the bottom was a man with a tool. The man put the wheel on studs which held it and the tool against the protruding studs. He then pressed a switch and the nuts went on smoothly. Even the tension was automatically regulated. When that was right the tool switched itself off. The man didn't reload the machine tool with nuts. Another man did that for him – Union rules.

And both men were graded semi-skilled. The Unions had forced that through.

This time there had been sardonic laughter. There was little unemployment here and most of the audience had traditional farming skills. They resented, though they seldom said so, that those alien oafs of the grimy Midlands should earn more money than they did and still complain.

. . . Perhaps that was worth a laugh, perhaps not. But it illustrated a deeper disease. That assembly plant had been uncompetitive. The line went too slowly, there were too many breaks. He, Clement Saint John, had made enquiries. In Germany there were coffee breaks too but the line went nine point two per cent faster. In Japan it was twelve and there were no breaks at all. And Japanese labour worked longer hours. We were paying ourselves too much for too little. Quite soon we should go hopelessly bust.

The audience was now shocked but attentive. From somewhere about its middle a voice asked courteously: "And what are you going to do about that?"

It had been an intelligent voice and Saint John answered accordingly. "I do not know," he said, "or not yet."

"A pity."

"A pity indeed but I won't soft soap you. There's

12

another party has all the old answers. It would throw money at the problem – lots of it. Inflate till it had to go cap in hand to the IMF. Like the last time. I can only say I think that's fatal. Some industries are already past saving. Shipbuilding and steel, for instance. Probably most textiles too. The peoples of the Pacific basin work harder than we do and live on less."

At the back a man had risen suddenly. "You're a Fascist," he shouted. "A Fascist pig."

It hadn't been a local voice and the meeting turned its collective head. The man was in fact a professional heckler and well paid by another party to heckle. The meeting looked at him, didn't like what it saw. "Siddahn," it roared. "Shuddup. Siddahn."

The man stayed standing and the candidate stared at him. "You were saying?" he enquired politely.

"I said you were a Fascist pig."

"You know what Fascist means?"

"Of course."

"With proper respect, and that isn't much, I doubt it. I do indeed. The word had a meaning once. Not now. It's vulgar abuse. It says you don't like what I'm saying – that's all."

The man hesitated for he was out of his depth; he had been hoping that someone would try to eject him. That he had been taught to exploit. Courteous, almost abstract argument was something outside the militants' curriculum. He looked around uncertainly and finally sat down.

Saint John asked the meeting: "Where was I? Before that."

A voice answered in the local Doric. "Talking about wages. Good stuff."

"I think I've said all I want about that. But there's another running sore and it's smellier. Foreign policy has been fiddled and fudged till you can't see the wood for the trees and the ivy. But basically it's as clear as day.

13

We're no longer a great power – let's admit it. But we do have a choice between two that are. One of them does silly things and its President makes senile blunders. I don't suggest we become its poodle and I don't want Trident; I think it's a nonsense. We'll cancel it next day when we get in. But that doesn't mean we'll opt the other way. In the long run that means simple serfdom."

There was a mutter of approval, then steady clapping. People began to rise, then all of them. Cheering began, then swelled in chorus. This was what they'd been waiting for for years. Good red meat and a plateful of it. They cheered till they were hoarse; they sang.

There'd been a man from central office present and he hadn't approved of the candidate's line; but he could recognise a sensational meeting. Clement Saint John had been asked to speak elsewhere.

The same thing happened, the same pattern exactly: first the astonished silence and scattered applause, then the storm of clapping and shouting. Triumph. Clement Saint John had become an asset. What he was saying was not party policy, or not the flag which the party dared to fly, but he could pack them in and make them stand to him. He had been asked to speak in a dozen constituencies, not the northern Labour fortresses where the doctrines of class war were too rooted and where he'd probably have been assaulted physically, but he'd torn great holes in the soft Tory belly in the south. His party got in with a tiny majority.

The bookmakers had lost much money for there'd been an undercurrent of sick discontent far stronger than either of the old parties had estimated. Things couldn't go on as they were and mustn't. It hadn't been a question of tactical voting but of a passionate desire for change. Any change. Anything was better than the old familiar faces, Red or Blue.

So he hadn't won the election alone, but it had given him much prestige in his party. Enough to make him

14

Prime Minister when the in-fighting ended in final stalemate. His party had been saying for years that it was ready for the reins of government. In fact it was no such thing by a mile. Tweedledum wouldn't serve under Tweedledee and only four others had ministerial experience. All these were renegades from other parties. One of them had grown pompous and slack on the pleasures of continental cooking and the other three were old and querulous.

The in-fighting had continued interminably, the Palace was getting distinctly impatient. Saint John's name had come up *faute de mieux*, been accepted. In astonishment he had inherited the highest office in the land.

As they turned right to go past the Treasury the guard quickened his stride and drew level again. The Prime Minister said in faint surprise:

"Want to talk again?"

"No, sir."

"Then what goes on?"

"Turning right-handed you cover directly."

"Part of the drill?"

"You could call it that."

Saint John made no answer since drills didn't interest him. His thoughts had turned to the Security Executive. He was its Chairman in any business which mattered, an arrangement which saved him reading minutes. Anything of real importance would come across his desk in any case and he much preferred to watch men's faces than to read their words reduced to paper. In his absence Lord George took the chair and did it well. The Prime Minister nodded. That had been an admirable appointment. Lord George had been Foreign Secretary in the government which had just been beaten and Saint John, who was short of experienced administrators, had been tempted to ask him to cross the floor, to go back to his old desk at the Foreign Office. But he had known that

n like Lord George would not renege. So he had
inted him Vice Chairman of the Security Executive.
George had successfully defended his seat in the
___se but had been frustrated in opposition and miser-
able. He had applied for the Chiltern Hundreds at once
and gone to the Executive gladly.

Yes, an admirable appointment – admirable. Foreign
affairs were meat and drink to the Executive, not the
foreign affairs of those dreary diplomats but the deadly
affairs of international terrorism. Lord George had had a
headstart on those. And of course he was Sara's brother.

But he was not. Many people thought he was for she
was much the same age and had the same Whig nose. In
fact he was her uncle by a whisker. Three days.

Saint John drew a mental family tree to get it straight.
The late Marquis had believed in enormous families and
had run through three wives in achieving his ambition.
Lady Mary had been his eldest daughter and Sara was
Lady Mary's child. Lord George had been the son of the
third wife. Lady Mary had died and her husband had
been killing two bottles a day. The Most Honourable
wouldn't stand for that, a drunken father and some
unknown nanny. He had insisted that Sara be sent to
Wykeham at once. He'd been a man who mostly got his
way and Sara had grown up with Lord George.

But appointing him had not been nepotism. Very far
from it: he ran a tight ship. And the others on the Board
were just as good. Jack Pallant, the Commissioner of
Metropolitan Police, formally known as Sir John – he
went without saying. You didn't achieve that office if you
were wet. And the man whose name had been shortened
to Milo. He was a Professor of Psychology in a respectable university and would turn his back if you called
him a psychiatrist. He was detested by all progressive
thinkers and had once been knocked down for quoting
the figures, comparing the IQs of black and white
children. If that was crude prejudice (Saint John kept

16

his own counsel) there was no other on the Executive's Board.

Which included William Wilberforce Smith, a West Indian of undoubted colour. He had been recruited by a previous chairman and had worked his way up from operative to the Board. At the time the appointment had raised many eyebrows, for in this sort of highly sensitive work would not a man of colour be exposed? Exposed to conflicting loyalties. But the doubts had been proven entirely groundless. Willy Smith was not ashamed of his race but neither did he flaunt it like a flag. He wasn't given to introspection but when he thought of himself, which was notably seldom, he thought of a professional-class Englishman whose skin happened to be black. He had also been to Harrow which helped. He was happily married, entirely assimilated.

A very good team indeed, the Prime Minister thought.

He turned his mind to this morning's agenda which was much as he'd expected it would be: the steady increase of organised terrorism and its danger to Very Eminent Persons. Those at the top could be guarded intensively though with modern weapons and suicide squads no sensible man could guarantee safety. And there was an insupportable crowd of minor Eminences who lived in the country, the softest of targets. There'd been a whisper, but so far only a whisper, of a parachute drop on one of their mansions. A suicide squad, of course. There wasn't an answer or not one known.

That bloody man they called the Maghrebi! Some people thought he was mad as a hare, but Milo had once defined him precisely. There were learned words, he'd explained, for men like that, but personally he preferred plain language. The Maghrebi was simply bloody-minded. Since he also had money and arms aplenty and the increasing power of fundamentalist Islam he was also the world's most dangerous man.

They had come to Birdcage Walk by now; they crossed

17

the road and turned left and left again. They were in the cul-de-sac of Queen Anne's Gate and although he had often seen it before Saint John slowed his pace to look again. It wasn't a style he particularly cared for and later accretions had not been successful. Nevertheless it was still impressive, an island of architectural sanity. In one of these solidly elegant houses the Executive had its discreet headquarters: offices for the very senior and a boardroom for the necessary meetings. Nothing of importance was kept here since nothing could be effectively done to make a house like this secure. The software and the occasional file, the occasional old-fashioned dossier, were kept in a modern fortress in Ealing, but a web of electronic wonders could put facts and often pictures too on a screen in Queen Anne's Gate within seconds.

The doorman said: "Good morning, Prime Minister," but he scrupulously checked the two passes.

The guard stayed downstairs in the porter's lobby and as the Prime Minister turned to the rickety lift he could see that the two men were making tea. The lift creaked and shuddered but climbed two stories. Opposite was a single door, another check. Saint John knocked and a voice said: "Come in, please."

Four men were sitting at a circular table and a fifth chair had been put there for Saint John. The floor was of ancient polished boards, uneven by now and, like the lift, creaking. They were covered by good but well-worn Persian rugs. The walls were hung with sporting prints and there was a single painting of a woman against a rustic background. She was handsome in her courtly way but not a woman with whom to take liberties. Lord George had once claimed that the painter was Kneller and if it was not it was close to his manner. On the opposite wall to the door stood a sideboard. It bore decanters and some fine old glass but none of the men at the table was drinking. At the end of the meeting there would be glasses of sherry, one or at the very most two. All these men were far too busy to dare to drink much before their luncheons.

As Saint John came in the four men rose. "Good morning, Prime Minister." They said it in chorus, including Lord George. In private he and Saint John used Christian names, but it would have been unseemly to have advertised the fact that they were related by marriage.

"Good morning, gentlemen." The Prime Minister took the empty chair.

The table was bare: there were no agenda papers. Each man had been shown one before the meeting, then all had been destroyed except one. "Item One," the Prime Minister said. "The Maghrebi."

There was a knock on the door and Saint John looked startled. The Board's meetings were never interrupted. He looked at Lord George in silent enquiry.

"The usual instructions were given, Prime Minister."

"Then it must be really important. Have him in."

A uniformed policeman came in smartly; he marched to the Commissioner and saluted like the ex-guardsman he was; he handed Pallant a long buff envelope, heavily sealed.

Sir John looked round. "You don't mind?"

"Of course not."

The Commissioner opened and read the message; he read it a second time before saying: "I'm afraid we must scrub the agenda, Prime Minister. Something rather nasty has happened."

"Not the Royals?"

"No, not them."

"Thank God for that."

"But the man called Petra—"

"Never heard of him," the Prime Minister said.

"But I have." It was Willy Smith. "The Maghrebi has threatened him more than once."

*

19

Doctor Petra was a conscientious practitioner in the unlovely town of Solihull. He had been born in Tripoli, half Italian, but had long since become a British citizen. He regretted missing the meeting that evening for he'd been chosen as the principal speaker. He held liberal views of a misty kind and he'd been going to lambast that upstart the Maghrebi. Military dictatorships were all wrong. Right and wrong were important words, immutable, and disguise it as you might (and the Maghrebi did) the fact remained there'd been a military coup and if his army turned against him he'd fall. But an elderly patient had suffered a stroke and that patient was also old and frail. To Doctor Petra the last two factors were decisive. He loved speaking in public, it was really his hobby, but if a patient was frail and poor he must put him first.

The student who was picking him up stopped his car in front of the doctor's house. It badly needed a coat of paint but the practice wasn't lucrative and what he didn't need to live sparely the good doctor gave away to charity. The surgery was on the bottom floor and the doctor lived above it alone.

The student rang the bell and waited; he heard the latch click as the doctor released it; he went upstairs.

He was surprised to see the doctor checking a medical bag. "An emergency," he explained. "I'll have to go."

"The meeting won't like it."

"They'll have to lump it. That woman of ours can speak instead." He added with his own wry humour: "She loves her own voice as much as I do."

"But it isn't such a good voice by a mile. She's good at abstractions, most of them fallacies, but she hasn't got the common touch. When you rant and rave – you must forgive me – when you say that the Maghrebi's a bastard—"

"He is. But I've got to see my patient just the same. You nip down to the meeting and make my apologies. I don't know how long I shall be with my patient so I'll take my own car and perhaps drop in later.''

The student went down to his own car sadly. 'That woman' was a solemn progressive: if you called her the Queen of Hampstead she would be pleased. If anything could embarrass a government she would certainly be there with the banners. But, though she tried to hide it, she was an egghead. She didn't have Petra's demotic drive.

The student started his engine, moving away, and a man from an upper window watched him. He could see that the student was driving alone but he wasn't a man of high intelligence and his orders had been clear and mandatory.

He pressed a button and the car disintegrated. The student hadn't suffered at all.

2

"The Maghrebi has threatened him more than once."

It was Willy Smith who had spoken promptly. Now he was a little embarrassed. He was the junior present and one mustn't be pushful. He awaited a gentle snub.

None came. The Prime Minister said amiably: "Tell us, then."

"The essential is that he isn't important. His power to harm the Maghrebi is nil."

"That's assuming it was the Maghrebi who went for him. We'll so assume. But if he isn't important why try to kill him?"

"The Maghrebi hates his guts."

"Again why?"

"Doctor Petra runs with a clique we know, the high-thinking and mostly futile progressives. He denounces the Maghrebi's set-up of course, but the Maghrebi is pretty used to that. But he also stands up and calls him a bastard. Which he is. An acknowledged bastard but his father was fond of him. He had him educated and then commissioned. The rest you know."

The Prime Minister considered this silently, said: "It sounds a little odd to me." He looked at Milo who was smoking a cigar. "How does it seem to you from your own strange world?" His voice had held no hint of irony. He was too civilised to think all psychologists charlatans, especially this man with the expensive cigar. His own profession disliked him fiercely since he spent much time in exposing its myths. To the Prime Minister this was reassuring.

Milo took his time in answering for he'd been following his own train of thought. He had been wondering if Clement Saint John knew – knew that he was having an affair with his wife. The Prime Minister was a tolerant man but Milo was a formal colleague. There were conventions and they'd been overstepped. That might grate more than the banal fact. He said at length:

"Not as odd as all that. Arabs are very touchy indeed about who begat them and who did not."

"But 'bastard' is almost a term of affection. When it isn't it's simply common abuse."

"Here it may be. Not in Islam."

"The Maghrebi has always claimed the right to avenge himself on his enemies anywhere. We've thrown most of his nationals out of the country, anyone under suspicion of being his man. It now looks as though we haven't gone far enough. I suppose we shall have to throw out the lot."

The Commissioner said: "We can't do that." He was wearing plain clothes and wearing them well. He was there because he was Commissioner of Metropolitan Police and at least half the evil which the Executive fought against took place within his police jurisdiction. But today he wasn't commanding police, he was talking quietly with distinguished colleagues. Uniform would be quite out of place, a matter of very poor taste, a gaffe.

The Commissioner said again: "We can't do that."

"Why not?"

"We'd have every *bon penseur* in the country onto our necks. If I may, I'd prefer to show you rather than talk." He spoke to Willy in an undertone and Willy picked up the phone on the table. He gave a brief order and put it down again. A screen on the opposite wall came alight. The picture rolled momentarily, then settled.

It was a tape of a disturbance in the street. It couldn't with reason be called a riot but there were a good many

23

police and a lot of shouting. The police weren't being stoned but they were being jostled.

"London," the Commissioner said. He pressed a button on a plastic console which Willy had put on the table before him. The tape stopped and a close-up replaced the general scene. Two women were carrying poles with a banner. One was very well dressed, the other scruffy. The banner read:

NO POLICE STATE HERE

"That's a friend of poor Petra's," Willy said. "Presumably the other is too. That's just the sort of thing she would jump at."

"And dress herself up to the nines to do it. Curious," Jack Pallant added, "the way that sort's mind works. That woman is disgustingly rich which weighs heavily on her social conscience. But she doesn't give it away to good works – oh dear, no. The lady is as mean as cat's piss. She takes it out on her late husband's money by joining every way-out movement. She'd rather be Queen of the Hampstead fairies than a good old-fashioned Lady Bountiful." The Commissioner looked at Milo, suddenly afraid he had gone too far. "Am I talking nonsense?"

"I wish you were."

Jack Pallant pressed a button again and the tape went on. The noise had increased and so had the tension. The Commissioner stopped it a second time. Now it showed two bearded oafs with another banner. This time the banner read:

JUSTICE FOR ALL

"Civil Righters," the Commissioner said. "Different but almost equally dangerous." This time he didn't explain or expand since he knew that his audience understood

24

him. Some Civil Righters were simple but genuine; they genuinely feared to lose hard-won liberties. But there were others who were far from simple; they were a conscious front for the Hard, Hard Left.

Which was ironical in its twisted way since when the Hard Left came to power these people would go first to the Camps. The well-educated fellow traveller was always the first to feel the iron. That had always happened before and always would.

Pallant switched the screen off and spoke. "You get the message, Prime Minister?"

"I get it loud and I get it clear. The people we threw out last year were suspected of being Maghrebi's men. We hadn't enough to bring them to court, nor might we have wished to if we had. And you've convincingly showed us what happened as a result. If we throw out what's left of the genuine students there's going to be very much worse than that."

"Which I shall have to contain as best I can. That little affair you've just seen was nothing. It cost a lot of police time which I could have used better, but no one was killed or severely injured. But if that protest had happened in other places it would have turned into a riot for certain."

"So we can't throw out all the Maghrebi's nationals and make sure?"

"Not if you don't want more serious trouble. A millstone of authentic martyrs or people who could be so presented."

Milo had been smoking quietly. Now he tapped off his ash and asked a question. "Why should we throw them all out?" he said.

The others turned their heads together. "You have something?" the Prime Minister asked.

"A hypothesis. We've assumed that this attempt on Petra was carried out on Maghrebi's orders. But we haven't assumed, or at least I haven't, that it was carried out by the Maghrebi's own men. We were thorough when we ejected the suspects."

"You're suggesting he used somebody else?"

"I'm suggesting the possibility – yes."

"From some other but sympathetic Arab state?"

"That wouldn't contradict my hypothesis. That was all I said it was."

The Commissioner asked: "But which one?"

"That's for you." It had been curt since Milo could be deliberately abrasive. The Commissioner flushed but controlled his resentment. He began to reflect aloud.

"The forensic people will not have had time to examine what's left of that car in detail but from the message I got it was a pretty big bang. Professional. That means a pretty big bomb. Not at all the sort of thing made from weedkiller and sugar in a shed. And I would guess there was also remote control. Since the Americans scored that near miss on the Maghrebi, security at ports and airports has been tighter than it's been in my lifetime. I don't think there'd be a very good chance of smuggling in a weapon like that."

"It could have been here for some time."

"Conceded."

"But I don't press the point," the Prime Minister said. "It isn't the sort of thing you find in a normal cache of arms. I think we must accept that it got through the net."

"But how?"

"In somebody's diplomatic bag." It had been Milo again and Saint John looked at him hard. Milo didn't flinch from his stare. "After all," he added, smoothly reasonable, "it was you who spoke of some other Arab state."

"Which could also have provided the men?"

"On the guess which we seem to be working on – certainly."

Lord George had been Foreign Secretary in the

government which Saint John had defeated. He turned to him now and asked simply: "Which one?"

"I do not know. There are too many candidates."

"Algeria?"

"A strong front runner but in this sort of race I wouldn't bet."

"But a bomb in a diplomatic bag—"

"It's perfectly possible. It's no secret that we now put them through scanners but there are explosives which can beat scanners or dogs. The Americans are trying to sell us a contraption which they claim detects anything but it isn't yet proven and we haven't yet bought it."

"I see," the Prime Minister said. "I see." He added unexpectedly, since the time was barely half past eleven: "I think we have earned a drink. Gin for me."

Willy, as the junior, brought it and the other three men helped themselves from the sideboard. The Commissioner and Lord George took sherry and Milo joined Saint John with gin. William Wilberforce Smith poured a glass of soda water. He never drank before lunch and sparingly after it. His drug, when he wished to relax or stimulate, was marihuana but not a lot of it. But of course he could neither smoke here nor wished to. He didn't even carry it but in the evening he and his wife would share just one. He had it under complete control as most Europeans used alcohol sensibly.

The Prime Minister drank half his gin. "If explosives can still get in, that's bad. If another Arab state is doing it we're in very serious trouble indeed." He caught Lord George's eye and asked: "Are Arab embassies under surveillance?"

"Discreetly – very discreetly indeed. If we stepped across the line there'd be a row. The Foreign Office would back it, too. The last PM loathed the way it worked and cut it down to size considerably. But the diplomatic club is still powerful. If one of them could half substantiate that we'd trespassed on his monstrous

27

privileges there'd be the sort of trouble you wouldn't wish to face."

The Prime Minister nodded since he wholly agreed. 'Monstrous privileges' had put it well. He considered all diplomacy otiose. Ambassadors, Ministers, Counsellors, Secretaries. These enormous establishments were entirely unnecessary. Many of the men who manned them were there as spies and behaved accordingly and the others who weren't misled their masters. They attended the same old round of functions, picking up gossip which they relayed home as fact. And modern communications, their ease and speed, had made of these men contemporary dinosaurs. What was wanted in every civilised country was a single but recognised representative who could be trusted to send home a message accurately. Then Junior Ministers would meet for discussion, possibly even for some sort of settlement. If the matter were too big it would move upstairs. Senior Ministers would meet in turn. Just occasionally if it were really serious the big guns would be wheeled out from their park. There'd be something absurdly called a summit.

That was what mostly happened anyway. There was no need of this cloud of pale intermediaries, characters from a Twenties novel, afternoon men. Perhaps they had changed from the Twenties but not enough. The whole system and the vast expense had survived on the back of a spurious tradition. In 1987 it was a sham.

The Prime Minister returned from reflection. "You were talking about stepping across the line. You were saying that if you did so there'd be a row. You also suggested I wouldn't face it. Gentlemen, you were wrong in that."

Sara woke Milo at six o'clock. He would have liked to sleep longer for he was honourably exhausted but he knew that he would not be allowed to do that. Sara, like the last Prime Minister, seemed to flourish on almost no sleep at all. Milo liked a generous eight hours, more if he was engaged in venery. He grunted but went to the kitchen and made tea. He fetched a table, went back to bed, and Sara poured.

"There's one thing we didn't discuss last night."

"I don't remember discussing anything."

He laughed. "You were in excellent form."

"Thank you. I return the compliment. But what was it that we didn't discuss?"

"Where you were last night and in fact were not."

"At Wykeham, of course. Where else?"

"I just thought I'd better know."

"Now you do."

Wykeham was the stately home where Sara had been brought up with Lord George. A half-brother, the present Marquis lived in a flat at the top with a boring wife. The rest of the house was open most days but had been spared the final indignity of a funfair where the park had been.

"Would Albert cover if somebody rang?" Albert was Wykeham's nominal owner.

"Albert would cover all right – I asked him. He may have descended to moths and butterflies but at heart I think he's a *roué manqué*. I think he's rather proud of me, the niece who has affairs all over. In a way it may make up for that awful wife."

It was the sort of remark which Milo mistrusted, straight from some book of pop psychiatry. He himself observed and measured, matters like IQs and reflexes, and if these led inexorably to unpopular conclusions he was quite prepared to face dislike from people whom he mostly despised. Psychiatry as generally practised was totally unfounded in science. In a decade it would be consigned to the dustbin along with the discredited remains of the pseudo-science which had once been phrenology.

But this wasn't the moment to start an argument. "Do you think your husband rang Wykeham to check?"

"I'm sure he didn't. My Clement knows."

"He's a tolerant man," Milo said.

"Not particularly. There are things which he detests and will try to smash – political shams, for instance, and doublespeak. He likes his sex when he happens to feel like it and when he does I see that he gets it. I don't make a middle-class fuss and hoo-hah because I'm fancying another man. No, I wouldn't call him consciously tolerant but in matters concerning the bed he's enlightened."

Milo lit a cigarette. He preferred cigars but not in his bedroom. He would have liked to sleep on but at least was in bed still. He wasn't in any hurry to leave it. He continued to question and Sara to answer.

"So you were supposed to be at Wykeham, were you? I wonder you didn't say the Old Rectory."

The Old Rectory was where Clement Saint John had been born in the days when a beneficed priest of the Church ranked one rung below the local squirearchy. It was where his father had dourly told him that he was just as good and maybe better than the lordlings up at Wykeham itself. Now the rector lived in an ugly bungalow and served (or didn't serve) at least three parishes. The Church Commissioners had sold the rectory and Clement Saint John and Sara had bought it cheaply as a place to escape to from London at weekends. They still used it as such since they both loathed Chequers.

Sara answered with a touch of impatience. She could read him very clearly by now: he wanted to keep her in bed and she wanted to rise. She'd had six hours' sleep and that was plenty. Her inexhaustible energy said: "Up."

"I didn't say the Old Rectory for a very good reason. When we aren't there ourselves there's only that couple. Both of them are pretty dim and I couldn't trust either

30

to cover up properly. Besides, we don't get down very often." She added with a touch of resentment: "Your people make that difficult nowadays."

"Not the Executive – the police. It's a terrible place to enforce security. It means moving armed policemen in coaches eighty miles. Even then it's uncomfortably open."

"Oh well." She moved in bed. "I'm going to get up."

He got up too and went to the dressing room. Sara hated to be watched as she dressed. She was forty-three, in the prime of her life, but she took some time to put her face on.

He showered and shaved and began to dress carefully. He was in his own flat and the day was Sunday. He chose grey flannels, white shirt and an open-necked pullover. But he put on proper shoes, not slippers, and a spotted silk scarf in the open shirt. He wasn't going out all day and there wasn't a need to dress other than casually, but he didn't approve of slopping about. It was too close to the loose thinking which he deplored.

He went to the kitchen and put breakfast together: five croissants in the oven to crisp, one for himself and four for Sara. He envied her her enormous appetite which never seemed to affect her figure. He himself had to watch his weight but she could eat what she liked and a good deal of it. She wasn't slim and she wasn't stout, a Venus de Milo before that regrettable accident. Milo chuckled. Venus de Milo. The thought had not been entirely fanciful for her father had had Greek blood in him somewhere and Greek women were traditionally amorous. Sara had an unashamed gusto, a huge appetite for what life could offer her. There were pejorative words for women like Sara but Milo considered them simply silly.

She came in and he watched her spread the butter. He had taken it out of the frig to soften.

Milo watched as she buttered her croissant, spreading

it like mortar, thick and firm. On top of it went strawberry jam. She took cream with her coffee and a spoonful of sugar. Milo ate his croissant dry. He supposed she must eat like that to keep going. Something must stoke her demonic energies.

When she had finished Sara burped happily. She put a hand up to do so but that was good manners. She wasn't ashamed of the burp in the least.

"You make a very good breakfast."

"Thank you. I try."

"You should eat when you're worried, it won't put weight on you."

"You think I'm worried?"

"I know you're worried. I can read you pretty well by now."

There wasn't any point in denying it. "We're all of us worried," he said. "All five of us."

"That affair of Doctor Petra?"

"How did you guess?"

"I read a newspaper. But I don't see why Doctor Petra should worry you. He isn't of the least importance and anyway they didn't get him."

"It's the 'they' which worries us."

"Come again?"

"Doctor Petra had insulted the Maghrebi who, being what he is, tried to kill him. But two months ago or a little more we threw out every single man whom we had reason to think was the Maghrebi's agent."

"He could have slipped in others."

"Possible but extremely difficult."

"Or used somebody else."

"Precisely what worries us."

"Contract killings," she said.

He was startled and showed it. The idea wasn't new when you looked at it coldly: if the Maghrebi were using hired killers he'd have to pay them. But she'd put it from a different angle. "Go on," he said.

32

"About what?"

"Contract killings."

She poured more coffee and thought before she spoke. "Contract killings would have one disadvantage – from the Maghrebi's point of view, I mean. It would rule out any sort of suicide squad, which isn't the sort to work for money. Men who take money to maim or murder want to live to enjoy what they've earned. Of course. And there's a disadvantage from your side too. A contract killer could be anybody whatever. You wouldn't have any line at all."

"That's just it. There's a convention in indifferent spy stories that you can walk into a pub in Soho and hire what they call a hit man over a beer. In fact it's a difficult thing to do. There are a few, a very few, pro assassins but they pick their jobs with exemplary care. The Maghrebi could offer unlimited money but they'd know he was already suspect. Therefore there'd be a line back to themselves. They'd be halfway to prison before they started."

She thought carefully before she spoke again. "The men who went for Petra may have been minnows but behind them would be a pretty big fish."

"But who else would have a motive?"

"Another Arab. A friendly Arab."

"This country is full of showy Arabs but not many of them think a lot of the Maghrebi."

"Perfectly true as a generalisation."

"Besides, the killer couldn't act alone. He'd need a master and an organisation. The big fish in fact. Any ideas about that?"

He hesitated but she wasn't a gossip. Moreover she was the Prime Minister's wife; finally, picking his words, he said:

"You're right about an organisation. We were throwing the idea about that it might be a formal one – officially recognised."

"A friendly Arab embassy?"

"Maybe. Or just a man inside one of them well disposed."

"That's all you've got to go on?"

"At present. We're sniffing about. But you know what embassies are—"

"I do. Make me some more coffee, please."

He made it neatly and quickly and returned to the table. She'd been thinking again as he'd been at the cooker. "As it happens I know an Arab diplomat. He's quite high up, in fact an ambassador. I met him at a dippy party. I don't often go to dippy dos but this one I couldn't get out of easily. Clement was going so I tagged along."

"May I ask which ambassador?"

She named the state.

Milo said at once: "Adam Khoury. I've met him too. But I can't think why they bother to keep him *en poste*. Nor how they raise the money to do it. His country is as broke as a deadbeat."

"He didn't look broke to me; he looked opulent. Beautiful clothes and expensive jewellery."

"He has a file like every other Excellency. It's secret, of course, but you don't go to coffee parties. In any case what I'm telling you you've seen. Adam Khoury lives very high. He's a Christian so he's allowed to drink and he's developed a very pretty taste in wine. I doubt if he also goes in for song but it's known he's extremely fond of women."

" 'Is known'," she said. "I like that a lot. It's something I can confirm, and do. At that party he made me a proposition. After five minutes chat an overt pass."

He didn't ask what happened; he thought he knew.

"No, I didn't jump into his arms at once. That isn't my form and you know it well. But I accepted an invitation to dinner. Tomorrow as it happens. At his embassy."

"You'll get laid," Milo said.

"That's perfectly possible. He's a handsome man but

34

there's something about him. I know he's a Christian but he's still an Arab . . . 'Woman is thy field. Go to it at thy pleasure.' That's typical of Arab thinking and it's insulting in two separate ways. And there's something about all Arab men which puts me off. They strut about in those beards and robes with villas full of wives and what have you; they try consciously to look madly male but there's something about them which gives them away. A certain . . ." She fished for a word and finally found it. "A puffiness," she said at last.

"I think I know what you mean but take care just the same. You'll be a woman alone and there may be servants."

"If you're thinking of rape I can take care of myself."

"Karate?" he enquired.

"Do I look like karate? I carry a gun."

"Licensed, I hope."

"No, it isn't licensed."

Milo was reading the banner headline. *Prime Minister's wife with unlicensed weapon.* But Sara wouldn't be interested in headlines.

"Where did you get it?"

"An American boyfriend. He was rich as sin but had lousy taste. I preferred the gun to unwearable jewellery."

He had recovered from surprise by now. "What sort of gun?"

"You won't approve of this – it's a toy. But you can carry it in your bag without feeling it or maybe put it where no gentleman looks. Of course it isn't much good for killing. You'd have to put it into a man's ear to be sure. Which you could do in an unwelcome bed." She laughed. "And those are the only circumstances in which I'd ever be tempted to kill a man."

"For Christ's sake take care," he said again.

"If I bed him I'll pump him dry of gen." She looked at Milo slyly, added: "You'd like that, wouldn't you?"

35

Milo didn't answer her.

"Answer me, man." It was wholly patrician.

"I suppose we would. Any information on Khoury—"

"Bah," she said. "You're all alike, you Security men. Anything for a line to work on. You're no better than superior pimps."

"I didn't ask. You volunteered."

"It's all the same. You'll do anything. Anything." Her moment of anger passed; she said: "Sorry."

"It's forgotten."

"And I'll probably just eat and walk away."

"Won't Khoury be rather offended – humiliated?"

"I don't care a curse if he dies of shame."

"But it might make a difference."

"What?"

"I don't know."

At the moment of this conversation, Adam Khoury had been drinking coffee when the message came out of the blue and felled him.

Return half a million or face the consequences.

3

Milo had a room at the Security Executive though he didn't use it every day. His regular work lay in his respected university and in the learned bodies which mostly disliked him. But this morning he wanted to talk to Willy Smith so he went to his room and cleared the desk briskly. Then he walked along to Willy.

"Good morning, Willy."

"Good morning, sir."

Forms of address in the Security Executive had been settled by long-standing usage. Everybody called the Prime Minister 'Prime Minister' and everybody called the Commissioner 'Commissioner' or, occasionally, being formal, Sir John. Everybody called Willy 'Willy'. But inside these general rules were refinements. The Prime Minister called Lord George 'Lord George' since he didn't wish to stress close relationship but the Commissioner who knew him socially addressed him by his Christian name alone. Milo was mostly called simply 'Milo', except by William Wilberforce Smith. Milo was twenty years older than Willy, a figure in his own strange world, and plain 'Milo' might have been over-familiar. But 'Mr Milo' was far too stuffy and had vaguely military overtones which were quite out of place in Queen Anne's Gate. So Willy called Milo 'Sir' just once and thereafter avoided direct address.

It would have made a thesis for some humourless sociologist.

Willy had been watching a screen but he turned it

37

off as Milo came in. Milo asked him now: "Was that anything interesting? If it was and I interrupted—"

"Not at all. Just a protest meeting supporting the PLO."

"They make me sick. They should be attacking the other Arabs, not Israel. It was the other Arabs who lost them their homelands."

"Not a popular point of view."

"Mine seldom are. I spend most of my time teaching people to think straight."

William Wilberforce Smith let that one go. Besides, he was a little puzzled. Milo hadn't dropped in to talk about Israel, a state which he admired but mistrusted; there was something else and he was finding it difficult. Willy Smith said:

"Would you like a drink? We may not keep it in our rooms but there's plenty in the boardroom upstairs."

"Thank you. A gin and tonic, please."

Willy went away to get it and Milo used the moment to think of him. Milo approved of Willy wholeheartedly for Willy had achieved the impossible; Willy had assimilated perfectly. He'd been appointed by the Executive's last head, the formidable Colonel Charles Russell, and at the time the appointment had been considered risky. But Russell had been an excellent judge of men. Willy had made it from operative to boardroom, in no way pushed by Russell, but on merit. No doubt he had had advantages but advantages without talent wouldn't have served. Still, there they were. Willy had been to a first-class school and showed it. He also had a comfortable income for his father had dabbled in property shrewdly, buying up houses in run-down areas, then, as the immigrants flooded in, letting rooms or flats at outrageous rents. Willy's father had been a cheerful rogue and Milo approved strongly of all men who bettered themselves.

Yes, Charles Russell had chosen extremely well. He too

had been a conscious realist, bending the law to serve his country, establishing the Executive's ethos. And something of his potent ego still lingered in the Executive physically. That bentwood hatstand in the corner, for instance. That had been his. Willy had clearly claimed it for himself.

Milo nodded again in approval of Willy. *Pius Aeneas*, he thought, and smiled. He admired the old, the unfashionable virtues, most of them at any rate, and filial piety was surely one of them.

Willy came back with the drinks on a tray. For Milo there was the gin and tonic and for Willy his usual glass of soda water. Milo took the gin and drank most of it. He put the glass down and began on his business. "At that meeting we left things rather up in the air."

"In the sense that we didn't decide on clear action. But there was talk of some friendly Arab state – friendly to the Maghrebi, I mean; there was talk of diplomatic bags; there was even talk of discreet surveillance of people who could raise hell if they found out."

Milo seemed to be changing the subject but wasn't. "Have you heard of a man called Adam Khoury?"

"All Excellencies have files as a matter of course."

"Is there anything of interest on his?"

"Nothing to connect him with terrorism. But it's known that he lives extremely high."

"So Sara Saint John was telling me last night." Milo looked at Willy straightly. "I suppose you've looked at my file here too?"

"I simply didn't hear that question."

"Oh very well – it isn't important. But Sara has met him too and says the same. He lives far beyond his salary or his *frais*. Perhaps he's rich; many diplomats are."

"He may have been once but I doubt it now. He's a Maronite: they've been shelled to pieces."

"But he lives beyond his apparent means."

"That's on the file and there it will stay. We couldn't

39

take that to the shirts in the Foreign Office. They'd be glad of the chance to tear us to pieces."

"But it's interesting."

"Of course it is. Any suspicion of highly placed persons interests the Executive professionally." It sounded pompous and Willy Smith knew it. And it was his turn to contribute something. Making it sound as casual as he could: "As it happens, I know Khoury myself."

"You never told me that."

"I'm telling you now. We were at school together, you see. Contemporaries."

"Have you been seeing him since?"

"Hardly at all. I don't move in diplomatic circles and he's had no reason to call on me here. But we sometimes meet at school high days and holidays. When he calls me Willy and I call him Adam."

"The old boy network?"

"As far as it stretches. Which in this case isn't all that far. Just as well since I owe Khoury a favour."

"A big one?"

"Between schoolboys, enormous."

"Better tell," Milo said.

"All right, I will." For once Willy was wishing he'd put gin in his soda. "At school we were both of us quite big cheeses. Khoury was a school bum, a school prefect. I never made that but I was captain of cricket."

"I knew that."

"Hold on. Khoury was in the eleven too. He was quick in the slips and could make runs at Number Six or Seven. But he started putting them down on the floor; he began to make no runs. I dropped him and he took it hard."

"That hardly sounds like your owing a favour."

"Wait a minute again – I hadn't finished. So one night I was having a drag up the chimney."

"The day you bowled Eton out before lunch?"

40

"You remember that?"

"Of course I remember. Wrong 'uns and flippers. They couldn't read either."

"Well, there I was on my back in the fireplace, celebrating a modest triumph in my own way—"

"Pot of course?"

"Of course it was pot."

"Where did you get it?"

"A girlfriend gave it me. Later I married her. We still smoke in the evenings sometimes but not a lot. Where was I?"

"Smoking hash up a Harrow chimney."

"So I was. And who comes in but Adam Khoury, a school prefect, no less, and a pretty strict one. And what does he do?"

"I know you weren't sacked."

"Thanks to Adam Khoury and that's what I owe him. He stands there for maybe half a minute, stiff as a rod. Then he wishes me good evening and walks away. I've never been able to work it out. Busting me would have been perfect revenge for dropping him from the school eleven."

"Not perfect," Milo said.

"What was that?"

"Khoury may be a Christian but he's still an Arab."

"That's too subtle for me."

"It isn't subtle at all. I've never treated a patient in my life, or only one. He was the son of an Arab prince and I fell for the money. He was totally degenerate, quite incurable, but I had every chance to observe him closely. That's what I do, you know – I observe and I quantify. It makes me unpopular in progressive circles which think of things as they wish they were. I don't pay attention to dreams or folklore."

"What's this to do with Khoury and me?"

"I was coming to that: it's about revenge. An English prefect would have peached at once. As you say, it

41

would have been perfect revenge. But an Arab wouldn't have thought like that."

"Why not?"

"Because the incident was accidental. He hadn't *planned* to catch you smoking pot. It wouldn't have been revenge at all. It wouldn't have been a satisfaction."

"Is that the way Khoury was thinking?"

"I'd bet on it."

"Very well; you're the expert. But I still owe Khoury a pretty big favour."

"Which one day he might call in."

"It's possible."

"I'm afraid for you, Willy Smith."

"But why? Charles Russell knew I smoked in private and Lord George knows too. Both of them probably wish I didn't but I'm as discreet as a District Nurse and neither much cares. Morally neither gives a fart. If I drank too much they'd have to sack me but taking a drag with my wife is something which goes." Willy smiled amiably. "And after all I'm black and they're civilised men."

The telephone rang on Willy's desk. "Excuse me," he said and picked it up. He listened in silence, said: "Very well. Tell him tomorrow at eleven. Good-bye."

He turned to Milo, his face unable to mask his surprise. "Adam Khoury," he said. "He wants to see me."

4

So Adam Khoury had been drinking coffee when the message came out of the blue and felled him.

He was the ambassador of a once civilised country which now couldn't be said to exist as a state. At least five militias prowled the streets of its cities and in its villages no man went unarmed. Two considerable areas were effectively controlled by foreign powers. The army couldn't be used lest it mutiny and the President's writ ran as far as his garden walls. Somewhere – no one knew precisely – was a UN presence of men in blue berets; it cowered or it ran away. Much of the capital city was rubble. Some days the airport was open, on others not.

Now Adam Khoury poured a glass of brandy, thinking brandy was rather a tricky drink. Take more than two and you tossed all night. Take four and you were drunk as you sat. This was Adam Khoury's second. As a Christian he could drink and was fond of it but also he could handle it sensibly.

His background was wealthy Maronite-Sunni, the old but mostly unspoken alliance which had ruled the country and made it prosperous. Or rather had made a part of it prosperous. Who cared about those wretched Shias festering in their slums like pigs? Who *had* cared, rather? Now it was different. This neglected, barely considered people had arms in its hands, a new spirit behind it. Islam had stirred in its sleep and claimed them.

And in doing so it had broken Khoury.

It had started with the PLO, the arrogant, treacherous PLO. When they'd stretched the patience of Jordan too far Khoury's country had given them refuge as honoured guests. When they'd promptly repeated their crime in Jordan, setting up a parallel state of their own, armed camps which their kindly hosts dare not enter. And they had gone on mounting raids against Israel, blowing up buses of children, murdering. It was terrorism of the ugliest kind and Khoury didn't approve of terrorism. Why should he when it had destroyed his patrimony? He thought of the shops, the blocks of flats, the hotels, all in the capital's fashionable quarter.

All gone.

He took a deliberate sip of the brandy. His coffee was cold but he'd had enough of it. He was surprised at what he'd been thinking but not ashamed.

He had caught himself wishing that Israel had won decisively, had destroyed its enemy, not merely dispersed it. But it had not. A few years ago on a memorable morning the Israeli army had stood at his capital's gates, ready to cut the city in two by a drive to the sea. It would crush the PLO for ever. But the Israeli army had failed to do that. Instead it had probed; met resistance; halted. Khoury did not blame the general concerned. Armour was useless in built-up areas and street-fighting very expensive in men. A half-trained guerilla with grenades and a pistol was too nearly a match for a fully trained soldier. The might of Israel had a single weakness. It couldn't afford to take serious casualties.

Khoury hadn't considered the thought a treason for he didn't think in terms of race. Pan-Arabism or a renascent Islam meant nothing to Adam Khoury whatever. Terrorism he considered pointless. Then why was he working for the man called the Maghrebi?

That was perfectly simple: he worked for the money.

Most boys of his class had been schooled in France but his father hadn't admired the French and had sent him to school in England instead. By the book he should have been quietly miserable; in fact he had been successful

44

and happy. He'd been westernised in tastes and culture but he wouldn't have needed a man like Milo to tell him that he still thought like an Arab. No man could cut his roots and stay sane.

His thoughts moved back to those rampant Israelis whom he supposed he should have hated but did not. After all it had not been Israeli guns which had shelled his patrimony into the ground; it had been the artillery of the various militias. He curled his lip in unspoken contempt, for the westernised side of Khoury was now in charge. The Beduin might fight well for their king but most other Arab armies were rubbish. They were good at sniping from sandbagged positions; they drove jeeps through the streets with recoilless rifles which they fired playfully at anything moving; they fired *feux de joie* for imagined victories; but anything like close combat they shunned. It was dangerous. Their favourite form of civil warfare was the artillery duel from prepared positions. But batteries didn't fire at each other – that might draw counter-fire and therefore was silly; they pounded residential areas, mercilessly, day in day out. Khoury had been back just once and people still lived in the broken ruins. There wasn't a dog or a cat to be seen. There hadn't been at Stalingrad either.

Khoury had wept, then Khoury had cursed; he had cursed all civil war comprehensively.

There was a knock on the door and a man came in quietly. He was a Second Secretary, one of only two staff left. The Minister and the Counsellor had been withdrawn. Khoury didn't like him much since he'd guessed that he was also a spy. A spy on himself, Adam Khoury, His Excellency.

Khoury's riven and broken land was that sort of country and always had been.

The Secretary asked: "Anything more, sir?"

"No, thank you. Go to bed. Sleep well."

The interruption had brought him back to the present,

45

from politics to Adam Khoury himself. The westernised Khoury disappeared.

He had done well in his Service, rising fast, and money had helped as it always did in diplomacy. Posts in capitals like the London embassy were seldom given to men without means. Now that easy life had turned bleakly against him. Milo and Willy had been perfectly right: his salary wouldn't support his way of life. As for his *frais* it was now derisory; it would barely cover the sort of dinner which he proposed to give Sara Saint John next evening. He thought of that with pleasure, confident, but the future as a whole was dim. His embassy had in effect been closed. The house in Knightsbridge was mostly empty and echoing; he had a Secretary whom he suspected of spying; his car had been taken away; he took taxis.

He cheered slightly at a single thought. He wouldn't be sacked or at least not yet. His country didn't exist as a state but no despised Shia would be sent to replace him. His family had lost everything, he was having to support his kin, but he still knew the ropes and would pull them shrewdly. The President was one of them and he wouldn't let Adam Khoury down; he wouldn't so long as Adam Khoury could contrive to save his official face, to keep this shell of an embassy just alive. But he would if Khoury publicly shamed him, went publicly bankrupt under a mountain of private debt.

But he wasn't yet bankrupt – very far from it. He had four hundred and fifty thousand pounds with a man called van der Louw in Belgium, safely laundered and as safely held. The Maghrebi's down payment had been half a million but he'd used fifty thousand to clear his urgent debts. And there was another half million to come when he'd finished off Petra. The Maghrebi was many evil things but he was generous with his parvenu money.

Adam Khoury laughed contemptuously. Like most

46

upper-class Arabs he thought little of the Maghrebi. He was an upstart who'd come to power from nothing, suspect of Moorish blood, even black, and he spoke Arabic with an appalling accent. The aristocrats of the Gulf wouldn't speak to him. Their own titles derived from their ancient religion. The Maghrebi was an usurper with money, a man who pursued a petty vendetta. Khoury took his money to do so. Why not?

It occurred to him that he hadn't yet earned it but he'd thought of that before and not worried. A mere accident had prevented success and Petra was absurdly vulnerable. Khoury could try again and would. Let the dust settle first, then plan afresh. The Maghrebi would agree with that. He was a badly spoilt child but he wasn't a fool.

Khoury was suddenly optimistic. He thought, inviting immediate hubris: I've got the down payment. Whatever happens I've still got that.

The Second Secretary came in again, handing Khoury a long envelope, open.

"I thought you'd gone to bed."

"I had. But this came in by hand. It's in code."

"Then you'd better decode it."

"I can't."

"Why not?"

"Only you hold that one."

"Then give it to me."

Khoury dismissed the Second Secretary-spy, walking to the safe in the wall. Something had clearly happened at home. It was probably another disaster but there was always an outside chance of improvement. Adam Khoury was feeling hopeful.

He had risen very fast in his Service but he had been through the appropriate grades. He knew how to decipher and deciphering's secret, which was never to read the words till you had them all. The first line was merely explanation: the message had come in from

47

another country and was being re-ciphered on by courtesy.

He looked at the rest and froze hard in his chair.

Return half a million or face the consequences.

He knew that he wouldn't sleep that night so that third final drink could be taken quite safely. As he poured it he saw that his hand was shaking. Some brandy fell on a rug on the floor.

In an indirect way the incident steadied him, bringing him back from the mists of fear to the need for an immediate action. For the rug had been a Turkish prayer mat and though its dyes were natural and mostly fast it might not stand neat spirit spilled on it. He went to the bathroom and soaked a towel, returning to try to wash out the stain. He did this three times and then sat down. He left the third brandy for he didn't now want it.

A very alarming message indeed and moreover inconveniently timed. For he had the outline of a second plan which would dispose of Doctor Petra finally, a brutally straightforward plan not dependant on bombing cars by radio. Should he now put his plan to Maghrebi and ask for time? He shook his head reluctantly. No. He was an Arab himself and he knew how their minds worked. In any choice between a simple plan and another of a Byzantine complexity they would choose the delights of the latter instinctively. Besides, he couldn't bring himself to bend the knee to a man he despised. And the soft option of returning the money was one which was no longer open. He had already spent a considerable part of it and the Maghrebi wouldn't accept part payment. His only hope was to ignore this message, to treat it as a sort of warning, the Maghrebi's idea of a Final Demand; his best chance was to complete his assignment, to continue as though nothing had happened.

But if it wasn't a warning but in fact a dismissal, if it really meant what it said and nothing more, then

48

Khoury, who couldn't return the half million, was in very serious personal danger. He couldn't foresee what form it would take. The Maghrebi's own men had been quietly expelled but if the Maghrebi could reach Doctor Petra through Khoury there was no evident reason, or none convincing, why he shouldn't reach Khoury through somebody else. Until Doctor Petra was safely dead Adam Khoury's life went on at the Maghrebi's whim. What he needed for the next few weeks was first-class protection and plenty of it.

He decided to drink the brandy after all. He knew where he could get protection, real protection of the highest order. He would get it from the Security Executive, from William Wilberforce Smith in person.

Who owed him an enormous favour.

Khoury had been more than half westernised but in the pinches he thought as his genes dictated. It didn't occur to Adam Khoury that a man in an official position might hesitate to use that position to repay what was a private debt. On the contrary his official position could only make the repayment easier.

He walked into Willy Smith's office next morning and Willy rose politely to meet him. "Good morning, Willy."

"Good morning, Ambassador."

Willy Smith was thinking privately that the 'Willy' had been out of context. It was acceptable on school occasions since at school they had been on Christian name terms and the unspoken motive of all school occasions was an itch to recapture the glitter of youth; but on a formal visit to a senior official it struck Willy as overplaying the hand. Whatever that might turn out to be. 'Mr Smith' would have sounded stuffy and 'Smith' would have been condescending. 'Good morning' alone would have done the job admirably. And Khoury was wearing an old school tie.

. . . Overdoing it again. I wonder . . .

They sat down together and there was a moment of

49

silence. Each man was quietly assessing the other. Khoury saw a handsome West Indian in a sober but well-cut suit which he wore with ease. On the bentwood hatstand hung a grey bowler hat and a rolled umbrella though the weather was fine. The lining of the hat would be spotless. Khoury gave a tiny sigh. It was one of entire satisfaction. This West Indian was now the essential Englishman and Khoury rather admired the English. They had characteristics which irritated an educated Arab – their addiction to sport could descend into childishness and it was hard to accept their absurd belief that the rest of the world somehow owed them a living – but they mostly kept their word and paid their debts.

He was confident Willy would pay his own.

Willy in turn had summed up Khoury. His clothes were expensive, his shoes hand made, but he wore them as though aware of their excellence. The inescapable word came to Willy finally. There was something about this worldly Excellency which could only be described as flashy. Willy asked at length:

"So what can I do for you?"

"You can give me protection."

Willy was astonished and showed it. "Protection?" he repeated. "From what?"

"Say rather from whom?"

"Very well. From whom?"

"From the Maghrebi," Khoury said at once.

He had rehearsed his story and how to tell it. Questions would be inevitable and it was a safe rule to tell as much truth as possible. So he had simply turned his story inside out.

As he'd expected Willy said nothing and Khoury went on. "The Maghrebi approached me with a proposition. You won't expect me to tell you the details but naturally the proposition was criminal. Equally naturally I turned it down flat. When I did so I got a threatening message."

"A specific threat?"

"Yes, pretty specific. It was do as I say or face the consequences."

"Alarming," Willy Smith admitted.

"I found it so. That's why I came to you."

"But why to us?"

"Because you're the best."

"That's flattering but a bit out of focus. It's certainly part of our odd little business to know who needs protection or soon may. But we don't provide it. We can't. We haven't the men."

"I think you could if you really wanted to."

"People have little idea what protection means. It means a twenty-four-hour watch in eight-hour shifts. That's three men at least and in some cases more. But the police would listen seriously, the more seriously if we recommended it. As we certainly should."

"I don't want to go to the police."

"Why not?"

"I'm a diplomat," Khoury said.

"So much the better. There's a special section of the Metropolitan Police whose business is to look after diplomats."

"I've heard of it," Adam Khoury said sourly.

"Anything against it?"

"Nothing. But equally no reason to trust them with my life." Khoury's expression had changed: Willy noticed it. He had an ace to play and was going to play it. "I came here wanting the best," he said, "and the best I intend to have or nothing. You have an excellent reason to grant it too."

There was no answer to this so Willy said nothing. Khoury sat stiffly on, watching Willy. He could see that he had understood him but also that he had stayed unmoved. The shaft had gone over his head into limbo.

The second lesson they taught a Levantine boy was how to control his facial muscles. At this moment Adam Khoury forgot it. His face showed anger first, then

51

disbelief. He gave Willy Smith a full minute and then rose. He did not offer his hand as he walked out.

In Birdcage Walk he found a taxi and directed it to his empty embassy. He resented that his official car had been withdrawn with the other symbols of Excellence but he was nursing a sharper resentment than that. For an Englishman had let him down, had denied an established obligation. With reservations he had admired the English. Now he had begun to mistrust them.

In the embassy the spy-Secretary approached him but he waved aside the routine papers. He was angry and sincerely hurt but he turned his mind to a compensation. For tonight he was dining with Sara Saint John and he hadn't the least doubt of the outcome. He had taken enormous pains with the dinner – too many if he had known her better. He allowed the first real smile of the day for it was going to be a magnificent evening. Sara Saint John was a splendid woman, a notable conquest for any man living. She was also a Prime Minister's wife.

One to remember. Yes indeed.

Sara Saint John had gone to Khoury with her mind more than half made up in his favour. She had appreciated his cool assurance, the firm invitation to dine at his home within minutes of an introduction. Many women would have taken umbrage but Sara Saint John was not of their number. There were those who were contemptuous of women who shared her pagan tastes but she was a granddaughter of a great Whig house and had inherited a wholesome indifference to the opinions of conventional persons. And she'd been powerfully attracted by Adam Khoury. She remembered that she had once told Milo that she didn't much care for Arab men; she didn't care for their extravagant robes, as out of place in a capital city as one of those professional Scots who walked down the Mall in a kilt and bonnet. Beneath those head-dresses would be balding pates and on the faces were theatrical beards carefully barbered to make their owners look macho. But Khoury had needed no trappings to make him male. He could stand on his own feet as that. He was a man of a different race but that hardly made him uncivilised. Sara Saint John had been sharply tempted.

But as the evening progressed the temptation blunted. Like Willy Smith a few hours before she began to feel that her host overdid things. He had received her in the ambassador's study and a waiter, clearly hired for the evening, had brought champagne in a bucket at once. Not that Khoury hadn't talked well and interestingly. It was natural that he should talk politics and she had feared that he might rant against Israel, cursing it for his country's collapse, damning the West for supporting an upstart state. But in fact he had been as detached as had Milo. The basic mistake, he had said (and meant it) had been his own country's and nobody else's. It had let in the PLO in compassion and the PLO had promptly betrayed its hosts. Everything had followed from that as inevitably as rain followed a thunderstorm. And what a storm it had been! The most westernised of Arab states now lying in fragmented ruins.

Sara had given high marks for this but had withdrawn them as they went in to dinner. She knew that Khoury's embassy no longer had a chef of its own and the dinner, like the attendant waiter, had clearly been brought in from outside. There was nothing wrong in that no doubt, but it need not have been so long or elaborate. And the *mise en scène* was quite simply corny: schmaltzy music in the background, more champagne. A third-class director's lame idea of what a classical seduction scene looked like.

Sara Saint John thought this very poor taste. A Whig lady was distinctly offended.

As the over-elaborate meal dragged on Sara watched Khoury with mounting interest and more than a hint of gentle amusement. She wasn't going to need the pistol tonight; it wasn't going to be rape. Why should it be? Khoury would have it all worked out, something out of some horrible handbook.

She tried to think as Khoury would be thinking . . . She was a woman of independent mind; she was known to have taken lovers more than once; and she'd accepted an invitation *à deux* on the very first occasion they had met. The technique in such cases would be firmly established. There wouldn't be any need of delicacy; the romantic approach would be a waste of time. What you did was to lay on a heavy meal and champagne by the gallon to wash it down. With the coffee would be liqueurs. Then you pounced.

The pounce, she thought. Method A-stroke-7.

The amusement had turned to distaste. Old hat.

And another unwelcome thought had swum into her consciousness. The technique to possess her might come out of some manual but was she in fact any more than a case in it? Was he aiming at pleasure or merely achievement? She was a woman of undoubted distinction, the wife of a Prime Minister to boot. She would certainly be one for the gamebook.

He was the sort of man who would keep a gamebook.

When the brandy came it arrived with some ceremony. The bottle was dark and appeared to be dusty, though whether the dust was genuine was something which Sara wouldn't have betted on. Khoury knew too much about spirits to murmur a reverential "Napoleon" but this bottle was undoubtedly old and Sara had drunk sufficient brandy to know what it would contain and that she would dislike it. It would be dark, almost viscous, and probably past its best. Sara preferred her brandy clear and light, almost as pale as a glass of good *fino*. It shouldn't be over-potent or burning but should go down with just a faint hint of fire. This spurious stuff merely wearied the bowels.

She declined it politely and considered her timing.

If this were the pounce, Method A-stroke-7, there wouldn't be much of preliminary dalliance, no time for a gentle disengagement, the approaches met with a shocked astonishment. Besides, she wasn't good at that. On the other hand to leave now would be rude.

Of the two she preferred the plain discourtesy. She finished her coffee, stood up and said:

"I'm afraid I must be going now."

He stood up too but not in acceptance. The action had been the simplest reflex: a woman was standing; he couldn't stay seated. She could see that he was surprised to the edge of shock. Finally he managed:

"I hoped . . ."

"So had I."

"I don't understand."

"Women may change their minds, you know."

This he accepted at once, without question. It was a cast-iron defence and no man could beat it. "I'll get your coat," he said.

"No, thank you." She didn't want him putting it on for her, standing close to her when she'd drunk champagne. She had begun to dislike him but he was still very male. No puffiness about this one after all. No.

She gave him more marks as she watched him recover. It took a minute perhaps but he did it successfully. Finally he said coolly: "So be it. You left your coat in the study, I think."

"I know the way."

He rang the bell. "I'll call a taxi."

"I brought my own car. It's still outside."

"Then it's probably clamped."

"Not outside what's still an embassy."

He contrived a formal smile at that and again she marked him up. But too late. He went to the door and opened it wide for her, standing by its side like a footman.

"Then thank you for a lovely evening."

"Thank you for your charming company."

She collected her coat and found her way out. It had been a lie that she'd brought her own car; she'd intended to stay.

She walked half a mile before finding a taxi. In it she let out her breath in a single sigh. She made a gesture of washing her hands but frowned. It had been the closest run thing since Waterloo.

The waiter would have gone home by now and Khoury turned out the lights in the pompous dining room, returning to his study and brandy. Not the brandy which he had offered Sara: that could go back to the wine merchant whence it had come. He poured his own which she would much have preferred, clean and vigorous with a hint of young life in it.

Now she had gone he could let himself tremble. Not in fear but in an increasing anger. Twice in one day, he thought – a single day. Willy had let him down – that was bad – and Sara had disappointed him too. The two incidents had had that in common but Sara had done much more than disappoint. What he felt was a total humiliation. She had played with him like a callow boy; she had taken him for the classic ride.

A mistrust of the English had turned to resentment.

5

William Wilberforce Smith, as in duty bound, had reported to his Vice-Chairman, Lord George. The two men got on extremely well for each admired the other's qualities. If Willy seldom thought of his colour Lord George never thought of his courtesy title. He was the last of an enormous family and his eldest sister, Sara's mother, could comfortably have been his own. This great Whig house had once been opulent but punitive duties had taken their toll and Lord George's father had been no more than rich. Even so with all those children on hand the Marquis was feeling the pinch or thought he was. The normal form for a younger son was Eton, the Guards and a job in the City but income hadn't stretched to that and the one thing this clan had never done was to sell property or land to make ends meet. Better to pull in one's belt a bit which meant skimping on the younger children.

So Lord George had had Eton but not the other two. As it happened he had wanted neither. He had been given a very modest allowance and on it had gone to live in Italy. To paint, he had explained, but professionally. The family had been surprised. Art was something one patronised not practised.

But Lord George had had a genuine talent and had started to sell in a difficult market when marriage had interrupted his prospects. He had met and married a very rich girl, the daughter of a major industrialist. She'd been ambitious but not in the world of painters and had persuaded him to return to England. Where he had gone into politics, again professionally, and in the last government had been Foreign Secretary. Willy Smith admired him greatly for he had the two essentially upper-class virtues: he was cunning and he was completely ruthless, innocent of middle-class conscience, the best Foreign Secretary since Bevin.

Willy told him his story and Lord George listened. At the end he said: "Let's take it *da capo*. At the last full meeting we risked three guesses. The first was that that attempt on Petra wasn't made by one of the Maghrebi's own men. Since we'd thrown out all the followers he had here our guess was that he'd found somebody else, but it wasn't supported by positive evidence. The second guess was also reasonable, that whoever he'd hired was another Arab. But we then proceeded to pure speculation – Arab diplomats and Arab embassies. And yesterday an Arab ambassador turns up in your office and asks for protection. You knew him at school so he came to you. Anything on his file of interest?"

"It's known that he throws his money about but it isn't known where that money comes from. He was a rich man once but isn't now. But he continues to live like an Edwardian prince."

"Edwardian prince is rather good. I know what you mean by Edwardian prince. And Khoury mentioned the Maghrebi by name?"

"He did," Willy said.

"That was significant."

"I'm not too sure. He'd have to tell a good story, wouldn't he?"

"He told a very good story indeed. I'd guess it was in fact a lie but like all good lies it was partly the truth. I was brought up in a competitive family where you had to lie well to survive at all. I'm a connoisseur of the competent lie."

"Why was this one so good?"

"Because it turned the truth inside out. The Maghrebi

is threatening Adam Khoury but not because he refused to work for him. He *accepted* the job of killing Petra, probably for a large sum of money. When he failed to do so the Maghrebi would kick."

"Another guess," Willy Smith said unhappily.

"The fourth as it happens. All pointing at Khoury."

"Actually the fifth."

"What was that?"

"I've put a very good man on Adam Khoury."

"That was a risk," the Vice-Chairman said.

"I remember what you said at that meeting." Willy's voice changed to quote Lord George's own. "'All Arab embassies are watched discreetly.'" His voice went back to his own as he went on. "We both of us know what that means in practice. A furniture van draws up outside one of them and we send a man to keep an eye on it. If it's furniture or maybe food there's nothing we want to do about that but if it's packing cases with foreign markings we start to take an active interest."

"That's about the size of it – diplomats are the great untouchables. But you've quoted me so I'll finish the context. I talked about a line in these matters. I said that if we stepped beyond it there'd be a row. You, Willy Smith, have stepped firmly across it."

"With a modest result," Willy Smith said modestly.

"Tell me at once."

"I was going to do so. Three obvious roughs have called at that embassy twice."

Lord George took time to consider this. "That could be conclusive – I mean against Khoury."

"Unhappily it is no such thing. These men were also Khoury's own nationals. They had a perfect right to go to his embassy and he a perfect right to receive them."

"How did they get here?"

"The simplest way possible. They stowed away on a ship and jumped it."

"Then we'd better get rid of them in double quick time."

"It isn't as easy as that, I'm afraid. They went straight to the local police and gave themselves up. They claimed to be political refugees."

Lord George, who'd been Foreign Secretary, groaned.

"Respectfully, I share your frustration. The fine tradition of British asylum has been stood on its head by You Know Who. There was a time when if you claimed asylum you had to show you'd done something political. Nowadays if you say you're political it seems to be accepted generally that the onus of proof lies on us to show that you're not. These men have no passports, they're here illegally, but if we just picked them up and sent them home there'd be a bigger row than finding out that I'd put a very good man on Khoury."

"I'm very much afraid you're right. So where do we go for honey now?"

Willy said cautiously: "I may have a line."

"This time you clear it with me."

"Very well. There used to be a cliché about *cherchez la femme*, and in some cases it was a pretty hot tip. In this case I think it's 'look for the money'."

"How Khoury lives as he does? Where it comes from?"

"You could put it like that."

"Risky," Lord George said reluctantly.

"Not so very. The money won't be in the United Kingdom and Switzerland is becoming unfashionable. But I thought I'd cast a fly in Belgium. Ostend to be precise."

"Any pointer?"

"A man called Stephen Palairet. He's a very big man in merchant banking, the head of his bank's whole network in the EEC. I knew him when I was in the same bank, before Charles Russell landed me here."

"And merchant bankers often hear things?"

"I was only a clerk but I learnt that quickly."

"Would he spill?"

"He might if he knows. He doesn't like Arabs in any form. He's a Jew."

"Then when are you going to start for Ostend?"

"As soon as I can – tomorrow morning. And I thought I'd take Amanda with me." Amanda was Willy's wife and a happy one. "She needs a holiday and she likes Ostend." Willy added as an afterthought: "Of course I shan't be charging her side of it."

Lord George began to laugh, then stopped. "Exemplary," he said. "Most scrupulous."

"If you mean I try to be honest, I do." Willy was only mildly offended: plenty of people put wives on the bill; but he added with a hint of reserve: "Charles Russell used to emphasise honesty."

"Colonel Charles Russell was right as usual. I'm sorry if I laughed out of turn. And reverting to your friend Mr Palairet: try not to drop a clanger."

"And if I do?"

The Vice-Chairman shrugged. "We've been quoting that last meeting freely, mostly what I said myself. I now propose to quote the Prime Minister." He didn't attempt to mimic the cool dry voice. " 'You were talking about stepping across the line. You were saying that if you did there'd be a row. You also said that I wouldn't face it. Gentlemen, you were wrong in that.' "

"Do you think he meant it?"

"Within reason – yes. Drop some silly brick causing grave embarrassment and he'd throw you back to me to discipline. But do something he thought was really necessary, something vital to the national interest, and he'd stand up in the House and brazen it out. Even if he had to resign."

"You think so?"

"I'm sure of it. Clement Saint John is vicarage bred, which means that he's a natural gentleman. I myself am

61

no such thing. By courtesy I'm a second-class noble-man."

"You got that one out of a play."

"More or less. At the time it was the line of the season; nowadays it would fall flat as a pancake. It was a joke about class and therefore taboo. Class isn't supposed to exist any more." Lord George looked up at Willy curiously. "But you, Willy Smith, can't have seen that play."

"They revived it on the box. I saw it with some other people. And you're right about nobody laughing."

"There's a lesson just the same – remember it. If you drop a clanger make it a big one. Go straight to the PM and confess it. If it's a little one and you come back to me I don't guarantee not to let you down."

"I don't believe that."

"I advise you to try to. I said I was a courtesy nobleman and we've had centuries of lying and cheating. Clement Saint John has not. Now off to Ostend and have a good holiday. The best restaurant, by the way, is the Chopin."

"I know it," Willy said.

"I thought you might."

Willy and Amanda Smith had been to Ostend before and had liked it. They liked its almost aggressive unflashi-ness, its air of a solid burgher prosperity; and English, not French, was its second language. Englishmen had come here to fight duels on the sands, men had settled here who had got into trouble, or gentlemen who couldn't live on their means. You still got further talking English than French: indeed if you looked unmistakably English and insisted on airing your French to a Fleming what you got would be a dirty look. Amanda Smith had been convent educated before she'd seduced Willy Smith and later married him. Her French was rather more than adequate but she'd learnt that it wasn't an asset in Ostend.

They did the things which variously pleased them and most of them they did together. They swam in the splendid sea-water pool. At this time of the year the sea would be tolerable but at low tide you walked a mile to reach it. They played squash which Willy treated as therapy. He put on weight if he didn't take exercise and Amanda who could owe him six would make him run till he'd had enough. The few things they did alone they enjoyed. Amanda would shop and buy their cold supper – their comfortable hotel had no restaurant for it was too sensible to compete with the good ones – and Willy would chance the casino occasionally. He wasn't a serious gambler but had one of that animal's characteristics. It was futile to set a fixed sum, win or lose. When you were out of luck you left but when you were on a streak you ran it. Lunch they invariably ate at the Chopin where the *sole flamande* was rightly famous. It was Willy Smith's considered opinion that most Belgians ate much better than most French.

Tonight he was dining with Stephen Palairet. Palairet had a house in Brussels but also this weekend flat in Ostend. The food had come in from outside as it always did but it was served by Palairet's well-trained manservant. Palairet had clearly prospered. Willy knew that he was still a bachelor but also that he didn't lack mistresses. They would be elegant women mostly married.

Willy had always admired and liked him. He was twenty years older than Willy Smith and had been halfway up his bank's strange ladder when Willy had joined it straight from school. And he'd seemed to be entirely unconscious that Willy was black, something near unique in the City. But Willy hadn't been pushed or privileged; when he'd done well he'd been quietly praised and when he'd made a mistake he'd been soundly berated. Palairet had treated him exactly as he had wished to be treated. It had been a pleasant surprise at the time but not now. For Willy, as he had matured, had understood. Willy was a Black who'd assimilated; Palairet was a Jew who'd done the same.

They had been talking first of matters indifferent: how the balance of wealth in Belgium had swung from south to north. The mines and steelworks of the south were finished but the light industries of the north were thriving. They were mostly backed by American money which could recognise good cheap labour and use it. It was the Walloons who were now the second-class citizens. But presently Palairet said:

"I can smell it."

"Smell what?"

"You're here on holiday but not entirely."

"In fact I came to pick your brains."

"My brains or what I might know?"

"The latter."

"It's true that in my trade one hears things." Willy noticed the 'trade' and it reassured him. Lesser bankers sometimes had tiresome affectations. They spoke of their 'profession', their 'clients', but the really big men still said 'trade' and 'customers'. Encouraged, Willy asked his first question. "Have you heard of a man called Adam Khoury?"

"The name rings a very faint bell."

"Then I'll ring it louder. He's an ambassador to the Court of St James's and by background he's a Maronite Christian."

"Oh them!" It was entirely contemptuous. "They asked for it and they got it. The Shias—"

Willy had heard this before from Milo but he listened politely till Palairet finished. "The only people there worth tuppence are the Druze in the mountains. They're yeoman farmers. Other Muslims detest them – they're mystics and a secret society. Which in Islam is a serious heresy. But they're industrious and give no trouble. There are thousands in Israel and all living peacefully."

"Returning," Willy said, "to Khoury—"

"I beg your pardon. What about Khoury?"

"His country is as broke as south Belgium and his embassy has been stripped to the bone. There's only himself and a Second Secretary. But he lives very well, very well indeed."

"Perhaps he's rich."

"He was but isn't."

"And you're curious where this money comes from?"

"Not exactly since we suspect we know." Willy Smith drew a careful breath, then said it. "It comes from the man they call the Maghrebi and it comes for services rendered. Dirty ones."

The older man was clearly interested. "An ambassador as a terrorist?"

"Not quite that. In this case the Maghrebi's pursuing a personal feud. One of his nationals, a Midland doctor. There was an attempt on his life by a car bomb. It failed."

"Trying to nail a diplomat is notoriously a frustrating job. But one of your several lines is money?"

"That's why I've come to you."

"I see." Stephen Palairet thought hard before he went on; at last he said with evident care: "We hold no money for Adam Khoury. That sounds like a breach of banking confidence but is not. It's a statement of general banking policy. We hold no Arab money of any kind. An Arab account is a constant headache. As customers they're far too volatile and they try to do you down over trifles. Normally they don't succeed but they waste a lot of valuable time. But if you're right that this Khoury has earned hot money it could very well be elsewhere in Belgium."

"In another bank?"

"I hardly think so. It's more likely to be held in trust."

"A trust?" Willy Smith repeated blankly. He was astonished and Stephen Palairet saw it. He smiled and said:

"No, not one in our sense. An English trust has two

65

well-defined parties. The man who holds the capital is considered to be the legal owner and the man who by law enjoys the income is called the beneficial owner. There are clear rights and duties on both sides. But in the sort of trust I'm talking about – I'm afraid there isn't another word – there aren't any rights or duties at all. The money has been simply made over."

"Sounds risky," Willy said.

"It is. The man who holds the money can welsh and you haven't any legal remedy. But consider the tax advantages, please. You can come to Belgium twice a year and return with your income as cash in your pocket. The Inland Revenue knows that this happens but it can't do very much to stop it. You could put up a very fair legal argument that that cash in your pocket is a gift *inter vivos*. It's tax evasion, of course, which is always illegal, but as far as I know there's been no test case. You'd be surprised at the number who use this fiddle and even more surprised who they are. Rich progressives who'd pull the world to pieces but jib at paying their legitimate taxes. Even an Anglican bishop."

"I can guess. But what happens when the depositor dies?"

"That depends on the man who holds the deposit. If he's honest he'll go on paying income to the heirs. If he isn't he'll simply pocket the capital."

"Has that ever happened?"

"Only once to my knowledge and a very small case. The system goes on thriving mightily and there are a dozen men in Belgium who work it. The biggest of them is called van der Louw."

Willy had been thinking quickly. "It's a very pretty fiddle indeed but I doubt if this Adam Khoury of ours is interested in tax evasion."

"So do I. But the system has another side and it's good old-fashioned red-hot money. When the Swiss began to ease up on their secrecy – I mean in cases where there'd patently been a crime – the really hot money came flooding in here and it went to people like van der Louw."

"You said he was the biggest. How big is that?"

"Rumour puts it at forty million at least."

Willy did some mental arithmetic. "Allow an average yield of eight per cent. That's thirty-two hundred thousand pounds to be distributed to the various customers. Less commission, of course. Say five per cent?"

"Nearer ten," Stephen Palairet said.

"All right, then – ten. So van der Louw's earnings are pretty considerable: three hundred and twenty thousand a year."

"That's about the size of it."

"But peanuts to the forty million. What happens if van der Louw disappears with it?"

"He wouldn't have to disappear – no smelly South American state for van der Louw. The money is his: it's been given him freely. Of course there'd be a resounding row; the government wouldn't like it all. A major default would kill the whole system dead overnight. That system brings in a good deal of money and a lot of it is invested in Belgium. There would probably be a financial crisis but if van der Louw chose to face it out I don't see how they could legally touch him."

"No CTT or its Belgian equivalent?"

For the first time Palairet showed a flash of annoyance, saying with an unnecessary precision: "Capital Transfer Tax is charged on a transfer. Here there has been no transfer when he cheats. The money is already van der Louw's."

"I'm surprised there's been only that one default. You mentioned just one, I think."

"I did."

Unexpectedly Palairet closed his eyes. The heavy lids came down like shutters. He dropped his head, then slowly raised it. When he opened his eyes his face had hardened."May I check on something you said before? You said that this Khoury worked for the Maghrebi. Criminal work, it was, and the Maghrebi paid him."

"We can't prove it—"

"Of course not. But you're not God's fools. And I detest what the Maghrebi stands for. He pays very well, though. Khoury could have the sort of money which would interest a man like van der Louw. There's a whisper in the streets and I'll pass it on. If this Khoury has money with van der Louw he is shortly going to find himself penniless."

He rose as he said it and held out his hand. Willy noticed that he had suddenly aged. The lines on the powerful face had deepened, he looked tired and even a little ill.

Open cheating disgusted him.

6

Adam Khoury had twisted and turned but he couldn't escape the barb which held him. *Return half a million or face the consequences.* Nothing could be clearer than that. It meant that he had failed in a contract and must therefore return the down payment. Or else. And he couldn't return the down payment – a lot had gone. Again he reflected that it was possible to clothe these bare words with meanings which made them look slightly less stark, but these were glosses and at heart Khoury knew it. His only slim hope was to complete his contract, when the Maghrebi might or might not lose interest in the fact that the first attempt on Petra had failed. He might even pay out the second half million, though that was in the lap of strange gods. Only one conclusion was possible.

Khoury would have given much of what was left to him with van der Louw for a word with the Maghrebi himself but he had no direct contact and couldn't arrange one. The bargain had been struck orally through an intermediary who had long since left London. The later message had been passed on in code but had presumably arrived *en clair*. His own Foreign Office must have raised its eyebrows and if he tried to send a message back would certainly do more than that. No, he must complete the job and pray that the Maghrebi act honourably.

That was going to need a powerful prayer.

But he did have a simple plan which he thought would work. No elaborate frills like radio-fired car bombs but an old-fashioned killing by shooting down. For that he needed both men and money and he tackled the money side of it first.

He rang up van der Louw in Brussels . . . Menheer van der Louw was not available but the head accountant was.

That would do.

The head accountant was cool and detached and his voice held a hint of what was almost indifference. He contrived to convey, though with perfect politeness, that Khoury wasn't a major customer . . . But of course if he wanted more money it would be sent at once. That same evening, and in cash? Yes, that was possible but would also be expensive. Air fares and reliable couriers were not to be had for nothing. And the accountant must remind Mr Khoury that the minimum balance was a quarter of a million. If it fell below that his House could not handle it and would have to ask for instructions to place it elsewhere.

It was all rather grand and a little chilling but Khoury had his money by seven o'clock.

He then summoned three men, though without much confidence. They were the three whom Willy had mentioned to Lord George and they had indeed jumped ship in an English port where they'd surrendered themselves and demanded asylum. But Khoury knew more about them than that. As their ambassador he had quite properly seen them and the more he had seen the less he had liked them. For in questioning he had learnt their story. They'd been members of one of two Shia militias and had committed the unforgivable sin. They had sold their weapons to another militia. They had been kangaroo courted and sentenced to death but had escaped and reached the harbour and a ship.

And now here they were in England up in the air. An organisation of notorious political busybodies was paying them just enough to live on and they had to report to the police every day.

Khoury looked them over doubtfully for they were

very poor material for a serious operation like murder. They were Shias from some festering slum, casual labourers who had been given weapons. He thought of them as Tom, Dick and Harry for that, to a man like Khoury, was what they were. All three of them were unbelievably stupid, though Dick showed occasional flashes of cunning.

Khoury started on his proposition, mentioning the money first. At once they shook their heads in unison; they demanded double but Khoury stood firm. He had deliberately made his offer generous and the demand for more was a peasant's reflex. Each man would get more than he could earn in a lifetime.

They muttered amongst themselves in bad Arabic and finally they nodded agreement. Dick then asked an expected question.

"But why should we do this murder and go to Brazil? We're going to be given asylum in England."

Khoury began to explain why they would not. They were in the hands of a certain organisation. (He had almost said 'clique' but stopped in time.) That organisation was extremely persistent in the pursuit of what it believed was rectitude but it had to have a good case to work on and their own was at the best rather doubtful. The tradition in this extraordinary country was freely to offer political asylum to those who were being politically persecuted. But who was persecuting Tom, Dick and Harry? Some other militia? That wouldn't wash. A certain sort of humanist might find their case emotionally attractive but officials, especially lawyer-officials, would stick in their toes and fight it bitterly. And knowing something of how the English thought, it wouldn't help that all three were bad soldiers. They had betrayed their own militia shamefully and they'd done it for a handful of money.

And deportation would not have agreeable consequences.

Khoury could see he was getting through to them; they'd be thinking that he was one of the privileged; he'd know very much more than they did about how things worked. He pressed his advantage.

By pulling a trigger once they'd have a brand new life and the money to live it. And the whole affair was absurdly simple; he had worked out the very few details himself. They weren't under any sort of surveillance so they could go up to Petra's town later tomorrow after reporting to the police as usual. There they would do what he'd explained with great patience, then get themselves to Manchester airport. Three seats had been reserved next day on the early flight. As for passports he was empowered to issue them; he had in fact already done so. The gun, then? He had one.

They muttered amongst themselves again and Harry said: "We haven't much English."

"You're not going to need a lot of English. One of you has enough." It was Dick.

Harry was still undecided and frightened. "I think I'll stay and take my chance here."

He saw at once he had spoken foolishly. The other two looked at him hard but said nothing. He wouldn't be allowed to stay, or not alive with the power of speech. Finally Harry shrugged but he nodded too.

Adam Khoury began to open drawers. From one of them he took a large envelope. It was sealed but not with the seal of the embassy. "The money," he said, "and also the tickets. If you wish to count the money you may."

The shook their heads and Dick managed a smile. The money would be all right. It had to be. If it wasn't they'd walk away. This man knew that.

Adam Khoury opened another drawer. "Three passports," he said, "and they're perfectly good ones. Issued at this embassy and valid for sufficient time to get yourselves settled down in Brazil." He put on a pair of washleather gloves before opening a final drawer. From it he produced a revolver. "This isn't on any British register. But don't try to get rid of it and above all things don't keep it yourselves. Just wipe it carefully and leave it behind."

When they had gone Khoury poured a drink. There was nothing to do now but wait. They were very poor material but the plan was of extreme simplicity. Doctor Petra was conscientious to a fault: if elderlies rang at night he went to them. Once that had saved his life but not this time.

Khoury had run through his plan more than once, hammering it home relentlessly. Its execution needed no skill whatever but setting the trap needed simple cunning. He had therefore chosen Dick to do it.

So next morning Dick went to Petra's surgery where he sat on a sofa and waited quietly. The receptionist, who didn't know him, saw him through her grille and came across . . . Had he an appointment? He waved his hands. Was he a new patient, then? He answered in Arabic. Finally she went back to her lobby. This stranger appeared to be some sort of Arab and her employer was an Arab himself. He could sort it out later, it was none of her business.

Presently he saw what he wanted: an elderly man on sticks, clearly frail. Dick waited till Petra had seen him, then followed him home. That was the only fear which Khoury had had – that Dick would contrive to bungle this. But the man with the sticks walked slowly and hesitatingly, intent on his difficult task of moving at all; he didn't look back and Dick followed him easily. He followed him to his Council flat and saw him in, then checked as Khoury had told him to . . . No, this wasn't protected accommodation – no porter and no warden's lodge visible. Also there was a telephone.

So far so good.

The three men went back there at two in the morning.

Khoury had told them what to look for. The habits of the elderly ran to an established pattern and they were very seldom security-conscious. Some even kept spare keys under doormats and many were careless in shutting windows. If luck were not with them in either of these they were to bang on the door and shout "police" loudly. The old man or woman would probably open. If they didn't they were to break in and risk the noise. Noise would increase the risk and cut their time but as a last resort they'd have to chance it.

In the event they found a window half open. The old man was asleep in a chair fully dressed. He hadn't been able to face the effort of getting himself to bed and up again.

They woke him in an evident terror – three dark men and one of them armed. He whimpered.

Dick had had a few words of English so Khoury had rehearsed him carefully in the few phrases he was going to need . . . He, the old man, had had a heart attack and Doctor Petra must come to see him at once. At first he appeared not to understand but Dick said it again and Tom waved the pistol. The old man shivered but reached for the telephone.

There was a conversation in incomprehensible English. One voice appeared to be answering in protest but the old man, under the pistol, insisted. Finally he put down the telephone.

Dick asked in his thick accent: "Good? The doctor is coming?"

The old man nodded. He was terrified but he wasn't broken. He looked at them with flaming hate.

They tied him to the chair where he sat, then they opened the front door from the inside. They left the light in the hall but themselves sat in darkness.

When Petra came in Tom shot him dead.

They looked at the old man in the chair. Khoury had given no orders to cover him: no orders had been faintly necessary. He couldn't be left behind to talk to the police.

Tom shot him too.

They wiped the gun clean and left it behind them. There were increasing sounds of movement from neighbouring flats and they left the old man's at a steady run. They had taken the doctor's keys and now took his car. They drove to Manchester airport fast.

Now they sat in line in the aircraft silently, trying not to look conspicuous. For at the airport they'd been badly frightened. There'd been an alert in force though not for them but they were swarthy and they were not well dressed. The machine had gone into gear at once. Their passports were barely three days old. Suspicious. A telephone call to the embassy followed and the Second Secretary-spy had answered . . . Yes, the documents were entirely in order. While this call was being made and answered they'd been put through the metal detector twice. Nothing had shown and they'd blessed Adam Khoury who had insisted that they leave the pistol. Their own instinct would have been to keep it. But Security had not been satisfied and they'd been subjected to a rigorous body search. Each man had had a body belt and in that belt a considerable sum.

More telephone calls had been made at once but the alert at the airport had been for bankrobbers and their appearances in no way tallied with the men who had caused the alert in the first place. In any case they had been trying to come in and not, as these three were, to leave. Exchange Control had lapsed some years ago and there was nothing in itself illegal in carrying a large sum of money. There'd been consultations with senior officers who'd been equally if not more suspicious but there'd been no bombs on their persons nor in their very small night-bags and the fact remained they were leaving the country.

Warn Rio, of course, but let them go.

So now they sat in a row, badly shaken. The flight had been delayed two hours but a stewardess came up to them, smiling. She was a big-bosomed girl with a faint hint of colour and they gave her that characteristic look, something between plain lust and instinctive contempt. If she noticed it she ignored it professionally. "Breakfast, gentlemen?"

They shook their heads. They weren't accustomed to heavy breakfasts and they'd had coffee at the airport already. But they did have a problem and they'd discussed it amongst themselves. They were going into a different life, into a different civilisation entirely; they couldn't afford to stand out by strange customs, they must do as the natives did to survive, and the sooner they started to copy the better. They owed a nominal allegiance to Islam but the flame of its renascence had left them cold. They had been born in a slum and had somehow survived in it till their sect had given them arms and hope. That hope had never set them afire as it had with many thousands like them. Their arms they had dishonourably sold. They were going into another life . . .

The stewardess said again more slowly: "What would you like for breakfast, please?"

"Bring us a bottle of wine at once."

7

The Security Executive was in session again, and since the matter was pressingly urgent Clement Saint John himself was in the chair. He had been showing the virtues which had swung an election, calling a spade a spade, never fluffing. Now he was recapitulating. The word 'recap' did not exist for him so Clement Saint John had carefully avoided it.

"I'm perfectly clear on two things at any rate. Adam Khoury takes money from that odious Maghrebi, his side of the bargain being murdering Petra. A low priority Arab feud but there it is. His first attempt failed but the second succeeded. Unhappily we cannot prove it. The three men he used are now in Brazil. It's just possible we could get them back, but the evidence of accomplices is rightly suspect. So the question is what do we do?"

There was silence. The obvious course wouldn't please the Prime Minister. Finally the Commissioner brought it out.

"We could declare him *non grata*."

"I don't like that. There are two main objections, one of them minor. I'll take that first. Khoury's country has no organised lobby here but it's been taking an almighty beating. To throw out its ambassador now could look like kicking a man when he's down and we might be charged with taking sides in a Near Eastern quarrel which isn't our own. The second objection is much more serious. The man is an ambassador, not some wretched attaché caught out spying, and no ambassador has been declared personally *non grata* since the mind of man runneth not to the contrary. There'd be an enormous diplomatic rumpus and if I have to face that I'd rather face it head on."

There was another and approving silence. The Prime Minister's views on the world of diplomacy might be unkindly described as a private hobby horse but most of the distinguished men present were prepared to share its saddle happily. The cool lawyer's voice went on impersonally.

"Why not? There's nothing in the law of this land says that a man who is also a diplomat may murder with a total impunity; only an international Convention, which in my view is out of date and a burden. We've had a shameful case of that quite recently and in my view it was handled weakly."

This time the silence was almost tangibly respectful. Somebody asked: "And the political aspect?"

"At home, you mean? I'd be ready to face it. There are plenty of Members who think as I do that the diplomatic bubble needs a prick. No doubt there would be some form of reprisals – selective expulsions, even embassies closed. But that wouldn't bother me. The diplomatic establishment is intolerably bloated." The Prime Minister smiled in faint apology. "Of course all this is academic since we don't have the evidence which we need for a trial. I mention it to make my point, that if we're going to ruffle the *chers collègues'* dovecotes I'd rather take a gun along with me. It would be an ugly skirmish and I'd rather have a proper battle."

The Commissioner said: "*Shabash!*"

"What was that?" The PM was used to the Commissioner's little linguistic idiosyncracies.

"An expression of complete agreement."

"Thank you. Then where do we go from here? Somebody's going to say it sometime so I suppose I'd better say it first. We can't leave Khoury at large and unchallenged. So far he has committed murder which you tell me was a private vendetta between the Maghrebi and the unfortunate Petra. Petra doesn't matter, the Maghrebi does. We've accepted that Khoury worked for the Maghrebi." Surprisingly the Prime Minister laughed. "Next time he might do something serious."

"We could frighten him," Milo said.

"But how? Put him on the mat at the FO? I don't think that would work for a moment. The Permanent Under-Secretary is a diplomat himself and a wet one. The Foreign Secretary is one of the few experienced men I inherited. He's conscientious and hard-working but nobody could call him formidable. Not at all the type to frighten Khoury."

Lord George, who had so far been silent, said tentatively: "I might have a shot at it."

"You? The Executive?"

"We do have a sort of weapon, you see. He's been to us once to ask for protection with an ingenious story we only half believed. The point is that if he came at all he couldn't have thought us entirely impotent. If he thought that we could concede protection he must have realised that we could invoke the opposite."

"I hadn't thought of that," Saint John said.

"It's by no means cast iron."

"Of course it isn't." The Prime Minister sounded resigned but decided. "Send for Khoury," he said. "Put him in the fear of God. More accurately of the Security Executive."

"I'll try."

Adam Khoury had been on the rack for some days for there hadn't been a word from the Maghrebi. He had not expected congratulation but he had expected some sign of acknowledgement that a contract had been duly completed. He had no way of contacting the Maghrebi directly but he did have a door to the way he was thinking. He rang up van der Louw at his office and insisted that he speak to him personally.

No, no second half million had arrived to his credit. On the contrary there had been a demand – from a source which he couldn't disclose but which Khoury would know – there had been a demand to return at once any balance which stood to Khoury's credit. Naturally it had been ignored. Good morning.

It had been curt but more than enough. Adam Khoury was now an expendable has-been.

He shivered though he was also sweating. He would have liked a drink but he had to think clearly. This he proceeded to do intently and he thought like the Levantine he was. He now needed protection more than ever. He had been to the Executive once and Willy Smith had shamefully let him down. Very well, he would go to the top, to Lord George himself. But Lord George might take the same line as Willy if Khoury approached him without a weapon.

Adam Khoury believed that he held a good one.

He wrote a request to Lord George for an interview, using the embassy's formal writing paper. It was thick and expensive and there wasn't much left of it. Then he sealed it with his official seal and sent for the Second Secretary-spy.

"Take that down to Queen Anne's Gate at once." No 'Please'. "You're to deliver it to Lord George in person. Accept no excuses – Lord George in person. This letter is very important indeed."

Evidently, the Second Secretary thought.

"I'm to take a taxi?"

"Of course. Why not?" The two men didn't like each other and His Excellency's manner showed it.

"I was enquiring who was going to pay for it."

"Take it out of the petty cash."

"There isn't any petty cash."

Khoury took out his pocket book and passed a

80

five-pound note contemptuously. The contempt did not escape his subordinate. "That won't get me back."

"I think it will. Take a bus or the tube or even walk." Adam Khoury risked a rare direct insult. "The walk will do you good. You're overweight."

In the taxi the Second Secretary laughed. He had information which his master hadn't.

8

Lord George had been told to summon Khoury and had been worrying about what excuse he should use to call him to his formidable presence. Ambassadors were not usually asked to present themselves at the Security Executive. He was therefore delighted to receive Khoury's letter, a self-invitation which solved his problem. He rang back and made an immediate appointment.

He then settled to prepare himself for he didn't wish to be caught wrong-footed. His time as Foreign Secretary had taught him something of the network of feuds, the inability to act collectively, which lay behind the boast 'Arab nation', and he had also met a fair number of Arabs. But these had been diplomatists and all diplomatists ran much to form. Of Arabs as people he knew very little. He had once visited an Arab country but that had been a conducted tour and its machinery had effectively insulated him from any real contact with ordinary men. He would have to let Khoury make the running, trying to meet his moves as he made them.

That was treacherous ground but there were one or two firm spots. Khoury would ask for protection again – that was as sure as anything could be – but the reason was a wide-open guess. When he'd approached Willy Smith he had told a good story, and, as they had said, like all good stories it had been partly true. The Maghrebi, Khoury had said, had approached him to commit a crime. Khoury had indignantly refused and the Maghrebi had reacted with threats. Well, now he *had* committed a crime, the Executive had agreed that unanimously, so why did he still need protection of any kind? There were two possible reasons, both of them guesses. Lord George wrote them down and considered them carefully.

Either the Maghrebi has something on Khoury, something more powerful than the offer of money, something he has had all along. In which case he may be demanding a second crime, something much more serious than the murder of a provincial doctor.

Or it may be a simple old-fashioned betrayal. Khoury has served his purpose and knows too much. In which case he's better out of the way.

Lord George re-read this and made up his mind. Of the two guesses he preferred the second. He might not know much about Arabs generally but on the Maghrebi he had an established file.

When Khoury came in Lord George rose to meet him. "Good morning, Ambassador."

"Good morning, Lord George."

"Please be seated."

"Thank you."

The moment of deliberate formality had given Lord George what he wanted most, a second to inspect Adam Khoury. He was faintly but fatally overdressed and there was something about him which wasn't quite genuine. For once Lord George risked an instant snap judgement. This was a westernised man but the westernisation was superficial. In any pinch he'd revert to his Arab roots.

"What can I do for you?"

"You can give me protection."

"Indeed?" Lord George contrived to sound genuinely surprised.

"You will know that I've been here before to ask for it. I knew Willy Smith at school so I went to him. He turned me down but I'm sure you will not."

Lord George was prepared to play this along so he repeated what Willy had said before, that if you read a rather dated thriller you received the entirely mistaken impression that protection was a matter of routine. In fact it was an operation which called for the sort of men and resources which the Executive had never had. He finished as Willy had finished before him.

"Why don't you go to the police? They've a special squad for protecting diplomats."

He was teasing. Khoury couldn't go to the police and Lord George knew it. For the police would want more than the general statement that this ambassador thought his life in danger . . . From whom? He had already told Willy that man was the Maghrebi so presumably he'd say so again.

Hm. The police would be making enquiries already into what was clearly the murder of Doctor Petra. They would know that three men had departed in urgency; that they were also Adam Khoury's nationals; and that he'd had contact with them more than once. Petra had been the Maghrebi's enemy yet here was the Maghrebi threatening Khoury.

Very odd indeed and a brand new line. No, the one place Khoury couldn't go was the police.

But Khoury was answering Lord George's question. "You were asking why I don't go to the police. The answer is simple. I do not choose to." His manner had hardened and Lord George noticed it. Adam Khoury had cards and he intended to play them. "You say you don't have the means to protect me?"

"That is what I said. It's a fact."

"But you've done it before."

"Who told you that?" The question had been involuntary and was regretted almost as soon as spoken. Lord George had conceded a trick unnecessarily.

"Another Ambassador."

The *chers collègues* again! How these butterflies chattered. But Lord George could trump this one and proceeded to do so. "Did your friend know the story – the whole story, I mean?"

84

"If he did he didn't tell me."

"Then I will." There was no harm in doing so: the matter was dead. "There was a diplomat in a certain embassy who had defected and spied for the CIA. When his own people found out he was in very grave danger. He came to us and we hid him away till the Americans could get him out finally. We hid him in what we call a safe house. Do you wish to spend an indefinite time in a villa in some run-down suburb?"

"I still think you could do better than that."

"And I'm telling you I cannot."

"Or won't."

"Take your pick."

"Then regretfully I shall have to insist."

Lord George took a grip on a rising anger. This interview wasn't running to form. He was supposed to be frightening Adam Khoury; instead Adam Khoury was openly threatening him. Khoury said casually, taking his time:

"Do you mind if I smoke?"

"You may smoke by all means but you'll have to find your own. I smoked once but I'm trying to kick it."

Khoury produced a gold cigarette case. Like everything else about the man it was slightly but noticeably over-elaborate. He lit his cigarette and said:

"One of your senior men is a drug addict."

Lord George's laugh was entirely authentic. "If one of our men were what you say we'd have spotted it long ago and acted. You can't use hard drugs for long and conceal it. The man would not have lasted another day."

"I didn't say hard drugs or imply it. It is enough that a man in a sensitive position should be using a drug which is still illegal."

"Marihuana, you mean?"

"You must make your own guess."

Lord George was back on the high ground and realised it. It didn't much matter how or why but this ambassador had somehow discovered that William Wilberforce

85

Smith smoked pot. But Lord George knew that and wasn't troubled. It was a possible source of official embarrassment but 'possible' was the word which mattered. Willy smoked with the greatest discretion and only at home. His wife smoked too and his mother-in-law supplied the three of them. She had a tolerated, almost respectable source, and pot was in the blood, a natural part of the culture of all three. Lord George would much have preferred not to know but he wasn't afraid of an imminent scandal. Khoury had got it badly misfocussed.

"I know you went to an English school and I know you've served some time in England. But I don't think you know how things work in a case like this. And I think I'll accept a cigarette."

Khoury offered one and with it his lighter. Gold again. Flashy. Lord George took a couple of pulls and coughed. He was almost clean and the smoke had caught him. He hadn't wanted the cigarette in the least; only a moment to think. This was going too fast. He ground the cigarette out and went on.

"To make any use of whatever you've got you'll have to go to the police and tell them. But pot is a drug which is widely used and some of its users might greatly surprise you. You could almost say that pot is tolerated provided it isn't used in public nor used to stir up a breach of the peace. As I admit it all too often is. So in a case like this the police won't rush in; they won't arrest this man of yours, particularly when they find out in due course that he happens to be one of mine too. Instead they'll make discreet enquiries . . . How much does he smoke and above all where? Does he smoke at home or with well-known troublemakers? Has he a quiet and reliable source or does he have to buy it on the streets? If the answers to all three are satisfactory I shall receive a call from a policeman, a Chief Superintendent as likely as not. We shall have a cosy chat and a drink and I'll promise to deal with the man concerned. The policeman will salute and forget it."

Khoury considered this for some time. "So you think you could smother it?"

"Since you use the word I'm sure I could smother it."

Adam Khoury rose at once. He didn't offer his hand but he bowed. In his taxi he swore softly in Arabic. His resentment had increased to dislike.

Lord George didn't swear but he thought very carefully. Khoury was becoming a nuisance and something must be done to abate it. But premature action was always foolish especially when he too had news which he didn't believe that Khoury had.

Not yet. When it came it would blow Adam Khoury to pieces.

Milo had made Sara's tea as usual and was now engaged in cooking her breakfast. As usual, he could have done with another hour's sleep at least but was otherwise in excellent heart, for he had an engagement that morning which he was relishing quietly. He was appearing at a literary luncheon. The gin would be second class and watered, the meal at some not too scrupulous restaurant. The fee would be derisory, but after the uneatable meal Doctor Ignatius Milovic would say a few words and answer questions. And a very rough ride they'd give him too.

Then why did he go? He smiled in self-knowledge, a little ruefully. Sara's husband had helped to swing an election by standing up and telling the truth. To Milo truth was something subjective but he enjoyed the sort of verbal war which he always won; he enjoyed sticking pins into pompous people. He enjoyed provocation.

So he'd rise and say his usual piece, aware that it would be total anathema. He would begin by pouring a detached sort of ridicule on what was currently the fashionable therapy. Strip away from it its pretentious jargon and what you were left with was basically dreams.

Well, witches, in the Middle Ages, had interpreted dreams to credulous peasants and had been burned alive at the stake for doing so. But the sham could not be dismissed, it had gone too deep. And it had powerful and noisy allies in the decaying world of knee-jerk humanism. Education, for instance – that was now a disaster. Mixed-race classes held back the gifted child. His own business was to observe and measure and he believed that Intelligence Quotients were susceptible to both. He had once been knocked down for stating his findings but that didn't prove that his findings were wrong.

Instantly there'd be furious uproar. The really big men in the literary world might belong to this club but they didn't attend it; they wouldn't turn out just to eat a bad luncheon. The man who got to his feet the first would be some novelist whom the press of the Left had blown up into a significant figure, but he wouldn't be selling enough to keep him. And after him would come a woman, somebody from the progressive twilight. Her name wouldn't matter: they were all indistinguishable. Her questions wouldn't be asked for answers: they'd be excited little diatribes directed at Doctor Milo in person.

. . . The address had been an outrage, a scandal. The Doctor was a blimp, a reactionary.

Milo, with an insulting patience, would explain that what he was was a scientist. His business was to observe and quantify and if the results didn't meet preconceptions that wasn't to be laid at his door.

. . . Then if he wasn't a reactionary he was clearly a racist. His remarks on education proved that. The Governors of his university had a duty to take immediate action.

But of course he was a racist. As far as he was concerned the difference between races was a fact. Low IQ children held back the brighter, and if you must see that in terms of race, do you know who protests the loudest against it? It's the Asians. Asians don't like their children held back in the name of an egalitarian dream.

Milo smiled again for he was a little ashamed of his taste for iconoclasm. But he thought it was no more disreputable than Willy Smith's pot smoking. Like Willy he had it in tight control. Like Sara with that toy gun of hers. In their different ways they were all discreet.

He returned to frying the eggs with some care. Sara liked them with the yolks unbroken and would ask him to do them again if he let them run.

When she came in he watched her eat. As ever what she ate would have kept him for twenty-four hours, assuming he could have got it down, but it never seemed to put an ounce on her. She was one of the lean kine, all right.

When she had finished he washed up neatly. He was a tidy man in habit as well as thought. Sara dried up and they went to the sitting room. Milo lit a cigar and Sara said:

"We were talking about Khoury last night."

It was a fact. Sara's husband told her most things since he valued her independent judgement; she saw men and events from a world which was not his own. And Milo was on the Executive's Board. Sara wasn't being insecure.

"We left it rather up in the air." That was a fact too.

Milo exhaled some cigar smoke thoughtfully. "Do you want to pursue it?"

"Yes, very much. I'm fascinated by Adam Khoury."

"Then if you went to one of the men I despise you wouldn't escape without hearing 'dichotomy'. Personally I think the word's meaningless. Or maybe it would be 'schizophrenic'. Schizophrenia is a recognisable medical condition but I don't think Adam Khoury suffers from it. I think he's simply a man on a tightrope."

"Who might fall either side?"

"Just so. One half of him is a westernised man who loves the good things which the West can offer. I suspect the other half hasn't changed from straight Arab."

"It's as good as certain he's committed a murder."

"He committed it for money, not from zeal. But there's a frightening lot of zeal around him. It's swishing round the Arab world like Arab money upsetting the markets. I told you I didn't know much about Arabs. The only one I observed at all closely was a degenerate princeling, which Khoury is not. I don't as a rule make generalisations but I saw enough of Arabs to risk one. They're very kittle cattle indeed. They can change overnight from love to hate."

"You mean he could fall off his rope to the way-out Left? Turn terrorist and start throwing bombs?"

"Not classical terrorism – certainly not. He isn't the type. Terrorists need conviction and training. Khoury has no training whatever and as for conviction I'm properly sceptical. He has distanced himself from Islamic fanaticism and in any case he isn't a Muslim. But if he does fall Left he'll do something sensational."

"And the motive?" Sara asked.

"There's the rub." Milo looked at her in admiration. She knew which questions to ask and which not. He put down his cigar and frowned. "This isn't the sort of talk I'm good at. I haven't observed and I haven't thought. But suppose this highly westernised man turned suddenly anti-West and all its works."

"Why should he do that?"

"I don't know. In any case 'West' was too big a word. Just suppose he turns anti-British and leave it at that."

"But why again?"

Milo picked up his cigar and drew on it. He was walking down his own street now; he'd been told the facts and began to recite them. "Milo is a Levantine Arab and face will be of supreme importance. We have spat on it on three occasions."

"When?"

"First when he went to Willy Smith. Willy turned him down with a bang though he owed him a considerable favour."

"Willy owed Khoury a favour?"

"Yes. But that's Willy's little secret, not mine."

Sara said: "I beg your pardon."

He looked at her again, admiration renewed. Say 'secret' to the average woman and she wouldn't rest till she'd wormed it out of you. The original conversation could go to hell. But Sara had apologised promptly.

. . . Clement Saint John was a lucky man.

He picked up his thread as though uninterrupted. "And the second was when you walked out on him cold. No protestations of outraged virtue. Nothing. You ate his dinner and walked away."

She laughed on a note which might just have been regret. "He gave me the feeling I wasn't a woman, just an entry in some private gamebook. But I can admit it was a close run thing."

"He wouldn't know that; he'd think you'd fooled him. What he'd feel would be humiliation. Which is something an Arab fears worse than a beating."

"I think you're probably right – he'd be squirming. And the third occasion we spat in his eye?"

"When he went over Willy's head to Lord George. What he feared was that the Maghrebi was after him and he wanted what he called protection. Willy had declined it once but this time Khoury waved a weapon. Or rather he thought he was waving a weapon. In the event your uncle disarmed him contemptuously and contempt is worse than humiliation."

Sara Saint John took a minute to think. "You believe those three would bring Khoury down – off that tightrope we were talking about?"

"I know men who would answer you Yes or No and do so with a shameless confidence. For myself I can only say I don't know. But those were three nasty balls in an ugly over and one or two more could easily turn him."

"Turn him into what?"

"An enemy."

9

Khoury had received a long instruction the substance of which had not surprised him though the way it had been sent had offended. Khoury was a shrewd professional and it had been obvious for several months that his embassy was no longer viable. Sooner or later it would have to be closed down, replaced by something much less pretentious, and that would mean a reposting for himself. So when these bleak facts appeared on paper he could accept them with the solid fortitude which expectation had nourished for some time.

But he hadn't liked the way they had been conveyed. For one thing the message had come *en clair*, which meant that other men would have read it, and those others included his own Second Secretary; and for another its tone had been almost curt. He had expected to be given a month in which to make new arrangements himself, but no, he was to return at once, and hand over to the Second Secretary who would take whatever action was necessary.

He considered his own position gloomily, the fresh posting which was now inevitable. It wouldn't be to another in the West, to a way of life which he would leave with a wrench. These posts were all held by men his seniors. They were safely entrenched and none near to retirement. There would shortly be a vacancy in a rich and reactionary Arab state but as a Christian he'd be an unlikely choice and in any case he would loathe to serve there. The contrast between the Western fleshpots and the grim rule of a puritanical sect would be very hard indeed to adjust to. So it would probably be South America where he had served in his younger days reluctantly. Or, if they had made their guesses, it might be serious and lasting demotion. In which case it would be some African stateling, or even, if they were really after him, suspected his sins but couldn't prove them, some noisy but impotent nuisance like Malta.

He wondered how much they really knew. He couldn't tell. In any case perhaps that was less important than it seemed. For his Foreign Office was no longer what it had been, a preserve of the ruling Christian-Sunni alliance. It had been penetrated by educated Shias. These men were few but they had caught the infection. Yes, that was the only word – infection. Simple or learned, starving or comfortable, to a man they dreamed of a reborn Islam. His Second Secretary was one of them. It was another reason for disliking him heartily.

So he had been thinking of his junior when the door opened quickly and he came in. He hadn't knocked. He took a chair and brought it to Khoury's desk, sitting down and lighting a cigarette. Khoury stared at him in offended outrage but he suppressed an inclination to reprimand. In the changed circumstances that would be futile. The Second Secretary said:

"So you've had it at last. You've really had it."

Khoury thought fast: there was no point in bush-beating. "You have read the latest orders?"

"I have. As it happens I saw them before you did. I was sent a draft and suggested some amendments."

"I knew you were a spy."

"I am. But not the sort of spy you guessed. I wasn't sent here to watch your private life, distasteful as I personally find it. I was sent to watch your official actions, to be able to assure my masters that you did nothing to prejudice our cause. Such as conniving with a Western power in making another attempt to intervene."

"I haven't done that."

"You haven't been asked to. If you were you would do what you could to help."

"You seem very sure of that."

"Of course. You're one of the old gang, aren't you? You're finished. You can manage an occasional kick but the future lies with us ineluctably."

Khoury had partly recovered his poise: it was time for a modest counter-attack. Besides, by asking a question himself he might pick up a little knowledge in doing so and knowledge was proverbially power. It was time to recover a grain of that.

"You spoke of a cause. What cause is that?"

"The sacred cause of the Arab nation." An evident and burning sincerity robbed the words of their offensive banality.

"And you think you can succeed in that? Against the establishment? Against the Americans?"

"Your establishment is falling to pieces and the Americans always get it wrong.'

"I'm obliged to admit you are probably right."

The Second Secretary's cigarette had gone out; he lit another and asked less sharply: "When were you last in our unfortunate country?"

"Two years ago; I didn't like what I saw. You could cross the Line then and I did. I wept."

For a moment the other's manner had softened but now his expression showed open contempt. Khoury would have wept all right but his tears would have been for all the wrong reasons. He wouldn't have wept for the human flotsam living in broken ruins like animals but for the loss of his own family's property, the hotels, the flats, the considerable patrimony. The Second Secretary reverted to harshness.

"You will find things greatly changed when you return. The political situation has altered."

"Don't tell me," Khoury said. He knew. The Americans

had tried to prop it, sending men and ships which had shelled open villages. The French had sent a small contingent, the British a squadron of obsolete armoured cars. But at the first sight of serious casualties they had run, their tails as low as an Indian dog's . . . 'If our men are there to fight they're too few. If they're there to be shot at they're far too many.' Admirable. But they had got it as wrong as they'd got Vietnam. Where they'd expected that firepower would give them a walkover. In his own country they hadn't even fought seriously.

And another power was in the wings, waiting to take that country over. It had always regarded it – Israel too – as part of its original territory and it had *firmans* from the days of Turkish rule to support this claim as a bare legality. But it was playing its cards, which were big, with skill. It wouldn't come blundering in like a police-man, trying to restore what had once been good order, shot at by all sides save maybe one. Instead it would watch and bide its time till one of the several militias came uppermost. Then it would take the winner under its wing. There'd be no open conquest, no accretion of territory, but Khoury's country would become a de-pendency.

His reflections were interrupted sharply by the man whom he realised was now his master. "It would be convenient if you were to leave at once. I have a ticket here." He handed it over.

"That's really very kind indeed."

The irony fell as flat as stale dough. "At the moment the airport is open. Take this chance."

"And if I do not?"

"You will meet with an accident." Now the voice held a very faint hint of pity. "But if you go quietly your position will not be entirely hopeless. Your people still hold the nominal levers of power. Perhaps they can do something for you, possibly not. But the President will receive you himself – that's normal with returning

Ambassadors. The formalities will be scrupulously observed."

This time the irony bit effectively. Khoury shrugged and asked: "Is that all?"

"Not quite. Another man may also send for you."

"Who's he?"

"The man to whom I have given allegiance, the man from whom we all take orders."

"The Pasha, you mean? So you're working for the biggest terrorist of all?"

"He's not a Pasha, he's as Arab as you or I. But somewhere he has Turkish blood and if he has a weakness it's one for flattery. Remember that if he ever sends for you."

"I think it very unlikely he will. If he's head of your organisation, your creed, then people like myself are his enemies."

"There's truth in that but not the whole of it. You have qualifications which he could use. You know the West, you've been wholly absorbed by it. I have friends who would call you a shameless renegade, but you're intelligent. And you know the diplomatic ropes."

"Qualifications perhaps, but why should I use them? Use them for a man I detest?"

"He might think he could turn you."

Anger restored to Adam Khoury a moment of his former authority. He had passed the offensive 'ineluctable', made no comment on 'the sacred cause', but 'turn' was too much for a sensitive ear. "You've been reading rather corny spy stories."

"Never a one but I've been trained as a spy. Turnings do happen and happen quite often. Sometimes a quite small thing can do it."

"What sort of man do you think I am?" He hadn't meant to ask it but it escaped.

"You're inviting insult."

"I don't care a damn."

The Second Secretary considered this seriously, saying in final, damning judgement: "I don't think I would call you a weak man but you haven't any kind of mainspring, no principle to hold you together. A psychologist would call you unstable."

"Oh, go to hell."

"To south London, actually. Where I shall try to be an efficient consul." He rose and walked to the door collectedly. At it he turned and said: "God go with you."

Khoury didn't answer him. There wasn't any conceivable answer.

Lord George had summoned Willy Smith to his presence but not to discuss his private pleasures. One of them had been used in an attempt to blackmail him, and though he had resented this he had brushed it aside with insulting confidence. As for smoking pot in principle, whether it was good or bad, Lord George had an aristocrat's total indifference. So he hadn't called up Willy to lecture him but to ask him for his considered opinion.

For the Executive had received good news and it was part of its established mystique that all good news, especially unexpected good news, should be examined with the greatest suspicion.

He gave Willy a chair and asked at once: "Have you heard of John Paget?"

"Our man in Adam Khoury's country?"

"That makes him sound like Graham Greene but it's near enough to the mark to pass. He has to be something special and he is. Our run-of-the-mill and resident snoop has the job of trying to pick things up. Whereupon he sends them here for assessment. Paget does exactly the opposite. In a country in its political death throes there's a rumour every five minutes or less and if he sent them all home we'd have to treble the filters. So he does his own assessment first and sends us only what he believes is important. The latest is that they've recalled Adam Khoury."

"They've found out what he's been up to and brought him home in disgrace?"

"There's no evidence of that, or not yet. They're simply shutting down that embassy. The thing is an enormous white elephant which a broken state cannot afford. A grand house in a prestigious street, a man who ranks as a full ambassador, but behind him a Second Secretary and a clerk. It's an evident nonsense they can't continue so they're going to close it down as an embassy. The house is Crown property but the lease has seventy years to run. I reckon that's worth a couple of million and with that they'll start something much more modest. There's enough trade with this country, enough of their nationals here, to justify some sort of consul. So they're buying a smaller house in Wimbledon – after all the Papal Nuncio lives there – and the Second Secretary will stay on as consul." Lord George paused for his second wind, then went on. "I suppose I should have seen this coming, but I don't pretend I did. Never mind. The arrangements which a fourth-rate state makes to have itself represented here are no business of the Security Executive. The fact that Khoury is going emphatically is. And it's come at a very convenient time. We're off the hook; we can sit back and watch."

"What will happen to Khoury?"

"I cannot foretell and I don't much care. Whatever happens to Adam Khoury he won't be coming back here to pester us."

"Pray for it," Willy said.

"Oh, I will. And I'll do better than that, a whole lot better. I'll have Paget keep a fatherly eye on him – see what he does and with whom he mixes." Lord George displayed a rare moment of anger. "The bastard waved what he thought was a stick at me." The flash of anger faded quickly into Lord George's customary Whig *realpolitik*.

"And I've a friend in his country who owes us a favour so I'll do what I can to fix him for good. We don't want him back in circulation. None of us does."

"No sir."

Sara Saint John was talking to Milo. "Have you heard what's happened to Khoury?"

"Of course. I gather that you've heard it too."

"Clement told me – he tells me most things. So that's the end of Adam Khoury. As far as we're concerned, I mean."

He took some time before he answered. "I wouldn't be too sure of that."

"What on earth can you mean? If there's one place he won't come back to it's here."

There was another and longer silence. At length: "I'm afraid I've got a hunch," Milo said.

"A hunch? Are you sickening? Hunches can't be measured or observed."

He was used to her occasional teases and his tone didn't change as he answered her soberly. "More accurately they can't be quantified. I confess I feel rather ashamed but there it is."

"I get hunches all the time."

"You're a woman."

"That's a very banal remark indeed. Since I get them all the time I discount them. When a man of your cast of mind gets a hunch it frightens me more than the trump of doom. Come clean – what is it?"

"It's disgracefully vague and entirely negative." He stirred his coffee and then asked uneasily: "You were saying we'd seen the last of Khoury?"

"That's more or less what I said."

"It's just that I wouldn't bet on that heavily."

99

10

The airport had indeed been open but the flight to it an uncomfortable nightmare. No major airline would risk a landing so Khoury had had to change at Athens. The shuttle to take him on was Greek, an ancient eight-seater which he could see needed servicing. The aircraft was licensed to carry eight passengers but today it was carrying twelve, four standing. Adam Khoury was one of those who stood, for he had lost in the ruthless free-for-all for the seat which was legitimately his. He stood wedged between other men and suitcases. The men were mostly unshaven or bearded and they looked at Khoury's expensive clothes with hate. Adam Khoury was apprehensive. Greek shipping had a poor record for safety and Greek aircraft were known to be flying coffins. This particular aircraft was overloaded and the pilot was wearing a boiler suit.

He gunned the two rough old engines harshly and the plane began to slip down the runway. It seemed to be slow in gathering speed and a silence fell on the noisy passengers. They were going to overshoot; they had had it. But finally they were somehow airborne and the interminable chatter returned to fray the nerves.

The pilot banked left, then straightened quickly, and they began to fly south-east with some purpose, never more than three thousand feet up at most. Below them were the classic Kyklades where warriors had fought and which poets had sung. Khoury had always found the myths boring. Presently, far to starboard, was Crete, and later, to port, a swift glimpse of Cyprus. The weather was fine, the conditions intolerable. The plane was making maybe two hundred knots. Later he saw his own coastline thankfully.

The pilot let her drift down gently as he sighted on the one runway still in use. A voice was squawking into his old-fashioned earphones but he didn't seem to be paying attention. Suddenly he pulled away sharply. The standing men were thrown in the others' laps. Khoury pulled himself upright by another man's shoulders and the other said on a garlic breath:

"The wheels, I suppose. He can't get them down."

"It isn't the wheels – they're not retractable."

"Then it must be something else."

It was indeed. As the pilot banked steeply the runway became visible. A coach was driving across it casually. Khoury's bowels turned to water and then to ice. He would have liked to relieve them but there wasn't a lavatory. In any case he couldn't have reached it.

The plane was now making its second approach and the man beside Khoury was praying audibly. There was a jarring thump as the wheels hit the tarmac, pitted by shellfire and carelessly patched, and the overloaded plane ran on. It ran on remorselessly for what seemed a lifetime till the brakes bit and it stopped at last. A single man brought a gantry indifferently. He didn't offer to help with the luggage.

They threw it out to take its chance, then walked with it to the crumbling terminal. Immigration was extremely severe and was conducted by uniformed soldiers, armed. The army couldn't be used lest it mutiny but took pleasure in treating travellers boorishly. One of the men who had travelled with Khoury was arrested and taken away by two soldiers. He didn't protest since he knew it was pointless. He'd be beaten up a bit and then released.

Beyond the official desks was nothing, an eerily empty concrete concourse, littered by broken booths and furniture. There were no newspapers, no food, no drink, but beyond the fallen doors was an ancient coach. It was the same which had almost destroyed them in landing. Under the ragged seats was a hold and the passengers fought to stow their baggage. There was a good deal of swearing and much confusion. Khoury was rudely pushed and once struck but after twenty minutes of chaos they lumbered away.

The coach took a route Khoury didn't know. The road to the airport was officially open, patrolled by peace-keeping troops of a neighbouring state, and one of the innumerable ceasefires had miraculously held for seven days. But the gunners of the two biggest militias had bracketed this road to a foot and at any time and for no known reason would bring it under murderous fire. Besides, the ceasefire had lasted a record week. It was due to blow at any minute now.

So the coach took a bumpy track across country into an area Khoury didn't recognise. It had presumably once been a straggling suburb but the bungalows and shacks were now flattened and cactus and weeds grew as tall as a man. Away to the west were the refugee camps. Adam Khoury hated the PLO, the proximate cause of his country's collapse, but for a second felt a pang of pity for the old men and women, the futureless children be-sieged in their intolerable ghetto by a militia which would murder them if it dared.

The wrecks of the buildings began to thicken and after an hour they reached a ruined square. Along each side was a row of taxis, each overseen by armed men in fatigues. Khoury fought for his luggage again and won it, then carried it to a Christian cab. He gave his address to the surly driver. The fare demanded was astronomical but halved when Khoury offered sterling. There was some further and distasteful bargaining – Khoury was more than sufficiently westernised to have lost any natural instinct for haggling – and finally they struck a price. They came to Khoury's home through side streets and Adam Khoury paid off the driver. He didn't tip and the driver cursed him.

It was a biggish house untouched by the fighting and Khoury climbed the fine steps which led to it. He rang the bell and nothing happened; he rang again, then pushed the door with his foot. To his surprise it opened freely and he went in.

He recoiled in shocked surprise and disgust for the entrance hall was now a shambles. The porter in his box had gone which didn't surprise Adam Khoury overly, but the rest of the considerable space was the sort of squalid scene he hated. Once there had been some good French furniture, a chandelier and flowers in vases. Now it was a communal junk room, littered by bicycles, prams and childrens' toys. There was a strong smell of cooking and boiling nappies and a line of these was hanging up to dry. He ducked under it and began to climb the stairs. As he did so a woman came down them silently. He didn't know her from Eve and she didn't greet him. He thought again and this time wryly of the Palestinians in their wretched camps. This might not be as bad as that but it was equally a ghetto under siege. It was the last refuge of the Khoury clan.

Outside his mother's door he hesitated for she hadn't been his favourite parent. As had been usual in his grandfather's time the marriage had been arranged successfully, a matching of wealth and social standing, but intelligence in a nubile girl had not been something which rated highly.

And there was another reason for hesitation since his mother's door was firmly shut. Normally she kept it open; she liked to know what was going on; she was very much the materfamilias. So if her door was shut there could be only one reason; she was talking to her priest whom he disliked. Adam Khoury knew that the emotion was mutual for on his holidays the priest had protested. The boy no longer went to church, he was acquiring western ways and habits of thought. Nothing good could conceivably come of that.

Adam Khoury smiled, for the second time wryly. Perhaps the priest had been right after all, for what had he got from the West that mattered? A love of its material trappings, the clothes, the brandy, the easy women; and the need to win the money which bought them even if that meant a murder. The priest's mistrust of the West had perhaps been right.

He let the priest go without accosting him and knocked on his mother's door.

"Come in."

He did so and was at once engulfed in a genuine but cloying affection. Her motherliness was almost Semitic. She wept and she called on her saints; she hugged him. He gave her a respectful kiss and, when the edge of emotion had blunted, found a chair. He had seen something he didn't like: a bed in his mother's day room. That was bad. Since her widowhood she had had two rooms.

He approached what he must ask obliquely: "As I came up the stairs I passed a woman. I've never seen her in my life. Who was she?"

"Was she carrying a shopping bag?"

"Yes."

"Then that would be Matilda."

"Who's she?"

"But you must remember Matilda." Madame Khoury was shocked. "She's the daughter of your father's first cousin."

"May I ask what she shops for?"

"What she can get which isn't much."

"Then how do you live?"

"We don't. We exist. Two of the men have jobs in the army – the real army not those wicked militias. It pays them miserably but they do bring it home. They get rations too and I think they steal others. I've a few pounds left for real emergencies."

"How long can this go on?"

"I don't know."

But she did, he thought – she knew very well. She'd had more than one reason for greeting him warmly. He was the only young male in the house with money.

Now he was more direct and asked: "How many people are actually living here?"

"Twenty-three," she said.

He didn't believe her. In the old days there had been nine at most: his father and mother, himself and a brother, since killed in a street brawl over nothing whatever, three sisters and two living-in servants. He did some mental arithmetic quickly. Nine from twenty-three was fourteen. "They must be sleeping three to a room."

"They are. It's terrible."

Something in her tone arrested him. It was terrible but there were compensations. She had always been the queen bee and enjoyed it. Now the flourishing hive was a slum but bigger. His mother was drawing comfort from that.

"Then whom am I going to share with?"

"Uncle George and that boy of his."

He remembered Uncle George with distaste. He wasn't in any sense an uncle but his father's very distant kinsman. He had been a small farmer and not a good one. Now his land had been simply taken away from him and the farm had not been sufficiently big nor Uncle George sufficiently prosperous for his own militia to risk a fight for it.

"I hope he's cleaner than when I last saw him."

"Now we mustn't be uncharitable, must we?"

The remark was one of unchallenged banality but he was a dutiful son and passed it dutifully. "I'll see what I can do to help."

"You're a very good boy. I knew you would."

There was an ominous note in this and he rose. He

was half reconciled to what he knew was inevitable: he would have to stay and care for these people, feed them, control their quarrels, *manage* them. Many of them were total strangers but all of them had claims of blood. He was the head of the family now. Inescapably. He was half reconciled but not entirely; he wasn't yet ready to put it in words and if he stayed his mother would wrench them from him.

He gave her another respectful peck and started to make his way to the door. Behind him he heard her voice again sharply:

"Leave the door wide open, please. People come in all the time to ask for things."

I'll bet they do, he thought but did not say.

He remembered something important and turned at the door. "Are there any letters for me?"

"Were you expecting one?"

It struck him as a silly question but again he let it go by without comment. If his future was what he had half decided he couldn't afford to quarrel with Mama. "Yes, I was expecting one."

"Important?"

"Very."

"Perhaps it will come tomorrow."

"I hope so." He did indeed, he thought, as he turned again. There was still a chance that they'd find him something. "I'm going to stretch my legs a bit. The flight was very cramped and uncomfortable."

"You'll be back for supper?"

"Of course I shall."

"You won't find it much."

"I'll bring something in."

He walked down the steps of the house and turned right. It was latish afternoon by now and the worst of the day's heat was over, but it was sticky and sultry still, bad for walking. He went slowly, looking around him, recalling. He was surprised how little damage there was

106

compared to what he had seen elsewhere, the ruins of his own flats and hotels, and this two years later after even more fighting. There were occasional gaps in the rows of neat villas where a Short or an Over had fallen incontinently but the area had escaped intensive fire. He wondered why and made his guess. This part of the town wasn't densely populated and it was people the gunners were after, not property. This area might be passing rich but this wasn't, or wasn't quite, a class war. It was a *jihad* against the unbeliever or the even more hated, the for ever damned heretic. It was killing that counted, not material damage. It was savagery to raise the hair on a man's nape.

The area might not be densely populated but in the evenings the housewives came out to the shops. One or two of these were shuttered, their owners caught on the wrong side of the Line, but others were open and uncomfortably crowded. He chose a butcher's and pushed his way in. He ordered a kilo of sausages – beef, of course. As a Christian it wasn't a sin to eat pork but only a foolish Christian would do so. In a climate like this pork meant a tapeworm and hosting a tapeworm could be extremely undignified. That, Adam Khoury reflected sourly, could apply in more than one sense. When the sausages came he looked at them doubtfully. A kilo had sounded a lot but it wasn't: it wouldn't even yield one meal each for twenty-three. He ordered three more and the butcher stared. "Are you buying for a hotel?" he asked.

"I'm afraid you could call it that."

"Why afraid?"

"Because my hotel doesn't make any money. On the contrary I have to keep it going."

The butcher was puzzled but made no comment. "I'll give you a carrier bag."

"Many thanks."

The cost of four kilos of very ordinary sausages had

come as a disagreeable shock, and as he left the shop with the carrier bag Adam Khoury began to think about money. He had a considerable sum in Belgium still but he wasn't sure exactly how much. He had had several drafts sent back to England and van der Louw would no doubt have charges. Against that there might be some earnings of interest, but he must get in touch with Belgium at once, arrange a proper portfolio of investments. And if the price of those sausages reflected costs generally then that portfolio must be one for income. Capital appreciation would be out. He would telephone tomorrow and fix it.

He was thinking of his money in Belgium, carrying four kilos of sausages, when a gun came into his back and a voice said: "Halt."

Adam Khoury stopped unquestioningly. He had heard that a gun in the back could be neutralised but he hadn't been trained in unarmed combat and there might be more than a single man. A car drew alongside and another got out of it. They bundled Adam Khoury in and one of them put a hood on his head. The first had thrown the sausages into his lap. Then he got in too and they drove away.

The two men were silent and so was Khoury. He couldn't see which way they were going but he knew that they had crossed the Line. There'd been a stop and an exchange of passwords, then silence again and the car had moved on.

Khoury shivered for he knew what was happening. He'd been kidnapped for money and he had only one source of it. That money was in Belgium but he groaned. He wondered how much pain he could stand before he signed that fatal order to van der Louw.

Almost none, he thought. He had lived too soft.

Behind him, on his own side of the Line, a man was scribbling hard in his notebook. He'd been a tail, not a guard, and he hadn't been armed. He'd been put on Khoury's tail by John Paget who had had Lord George's clear instructions.

He had the make of the car and the number too, though he didn't suppose that that was genuine. But what he had seen he had not expected and he was recording it while he remembered the detail. John Paget paid his legmen well.

11

The speed of the car had come down to a crawl as it bumped across the smaller shell holes, made wide detours to avoid the bigger. Finally the car stopped abruptly. The man on Khoury's right took his hood off and the man on his left got down and held the door. "Be careful, please," he said. "Your sight may be affected by that hood." His manner was courteous, even considerate.

Khoury stood on the pavement, blinking uncertainly. Under the hood he'd been as blind as a bat and in the early evening the light was still strong. He hadn't the least idea where he was: it might have been almost anywhere in an area which had been mercilessly pounded. Most of the houses were shells or rubble and opposite where they'd stopped was a little park. Copies of classical statues, headless, lay forlornly in the untended parterres and the fountain in the middle was broken and dry. But one house, though it had lost its top storey, apparently still held human life for a man was standing motionless on its steps. He was a curious figure and Khoury stared. He wore black trousers and a striped waistcoat with sleeves. These gave him the air of a liveried servant but across his chest hung a modern machine pistol. "Come with us, please," the two men said together.

Khoury obeyed. There was another exchange with the man with the pistol, then all three of them went into the house. It was shuttered and after the sunlight Stygian, and one of the men flicked a switch on the wall. No light came on and he clucked in annoyance. "Silly of me," he said. "I'd forgotten." They felt their way up an unswept staircase and stopped before a closed door. One man knocked. Told to come in he threw it wide, then all three of them stepped back respectfully. The shutters of this room were open and Khoury could see a big man behind a desk. He rose as he saw Khoury and raised a hand. There was a radio on his desk and he'd been using it.

"The driver says you were carrying sausages. They will go into the icebox at once. Without current the frig doesn't work, of course, but I've connections and I sometimes get ice. Please sit down."

If this greeting had been intended to reassure it succeeded. Undoubtedly this affair was a kidnap but it seemed to be a very gentle one. They would hardly bother with Khoury's sausages if they intended to hold his person indefinitely. He took the chair which the big man had waved at and inspected him across the desk. His face was lean but his body enormous. He must have weighed over two hundred pounds but the fat was hard fat like the wrestler's which he once had been. He was clean shaven and wore his grey hair *en brosse*. The blood of some distant Crusading knight had endowed him with eyes of a startling blue.

He bore Khoury's inspection without resentment: evidently he was used to stares. Finally he said politely: "They call me the Pasha but quite absurdly. It's true that I have Turkish blood somewhere but I don't believe it was Pasha class."

"I have heard of you," Khoury said. "Who hasn't?"

"You flatter me but there it is. And I think your Second Secretary mentioned that when you got back here I might want to see you."

"I realised he was an agent but not for whom. Till he let it slip out, that is."

"He was told to. For improbable as it must have seemed at the time I did and I still do want to talk to you. For several good reasons which we'll come to later. For the moment please accept my apologies for the means I had to use to meet you. You will realise that I had no other and I hope that the journey was not too uncomfortable."

"I was frightened," Khoury said.

The Pasha laughed. He had all his own teeth and showed them confidently. "I should have been frightened too, but permit me to reassure you formally. When we've had our little talk you'll be taken home."

A servant brought in Turkish coffee, pouring it into cups from a brass pan. "So let's start with myself – I present my credentials. It's widely believed I'm a terrorist boss but that's a little wide of the mark. I was a terrorist once in my modest way and I've kept the terrorist's faith undiminished. But I'm too old for the field and much too stout." He added but without ill feeling: "As you've no doubt observed for yourself by now. So I'm no longer an active terrorist but you could call me a sort of terrorist broker. Somebody thinks up an act of terrorism and they come to me to put flesh on the bones. I have plenty of men who'll accept my orders and excellent sources of information. The money I get from the same source as you did."

The Pasha sat back and waited patiently; he knew that the words would shock severely and he could see that the blow had in fact struck hard. Khoury for his part was trying to think straight. Finally he asked uncertainly:

"You are warning me?"

"Yes. But not of the Maghrebi. The Maghrebi is a vengeful man or he wouldn't have hired you to kill Doctor Petra. You made rather a mess of a simple job and naturally he isn't pleased with you. I've even heard whispers that you asked for protection. But that was overdoing it grossly. The Maghrebi would pursue a spent agent but only if he thought it necessary. In your case I don't think he will. Why should he? You have a dangerous secret but no motive to blow it. More important, perhaps, there is no one to buy it. Nevertheless

112

you've been shadowed closely from the minute you stepped off that horrible aircraft. But not by the Maghrebi's
men. Oh no."

"Then by whom?"

"By the British."

"But why?" Khoury was feeling increasingly uneasy.

For the first time the Pasha showed irritation. "Oh
come. The British will have it in for you – hard. They will
know, short of proof, that you murdered Petra and their
Security doesn't like loose ends. They'll be interested in
your contacts here – above all that you never return to
London. They have a very good man here to do just
that."

"Then talking of contacts—"

"I see what you mean. You were being tailed when I
was obliged to snatch you but you couldn't have been
followed here across the Line. The snatch could have
been of the usual kind, for ransom or the release of some
prisoner. But they won't think that when they see you
return tonight. They'll start guessing who snatched you
just to talk."

"Is that bad?"

"For me? Not at all. The British cannot touch me here
nor, for that matter, anywhere else. But it might be bad
for you if they guess right."

"You think they will?"

"I told you they had a very good man here."

. . . So you knowingly increased my risks by bringing
me here when you knew I was followed . . .

The Pasha read the thought unerringly. "I had another
and better reason for meeting you. I think you are a
wasted man."

It was a curious phrase and Khoury was interested. He
was angry but he was prepared to listen. "Wasted in
what way?" he asked.

"You have no roots."

"You are very wrong. My roots are here with my

113

miserable family. I still have some money – what the Maghrebi tried to get back but didn't. I have it held where I don't think he'll touch it. I shall use it to feed the mouths I must."

"Very proper," the Pasha said. "Very dutiful." He spoke sincerely and with a real respect. "But I don't think it will last for long."

"The money you mean?"

"No, I meant yourself. You're too intelligent to be running a boarding house." He was silent for nearly a minute, then said: "The other reason I brought you here was to offer you a job. If I found you ripe."

"But I'm no sort of terrorist."

"That I know." The Pasha's manner had subtly changed and Khoury, who was quick, had noticed it. Up to now he had been speaking coolly, almost with a hint of levity, as though he were talking to please himself. Now he said with a sudden and naked passion:

"*I hate the West.*"

"I don't much like the West myself. Look what it has done to us everywhere."

"I don't suggest you're consciously lying but I think that you deceive yourself pitiably. You admire the West, you've acquired its habits. You're its prisoner, it has stolen your manhood." The Pasha had begun to sweat; he wiped his forehead and then his hands. "If only you had Grace," he said.

"I'm a Maronite. We accept God's Grace."

"I didn't mean that sort of Grace. I meant a simple commitment to reborn Islam—"

. . . Oh God, I'm getting that again.

"—which you do not have so I cannot employ you."

"Would you ever have used a Christian?"

"Why not? Given he had the same motive as I have it needn't have come from religious conviction. As it happens I have that too as well as hate. I'm a Druze, you see."

114

"I didn't know that."

"Very few people do, and designedly. The Druze are mystics and we're a secret society. We believe we hold truth and we guard it zealously; we're as Quietist as the original Quakers – you could call it a sort of protective skin. We take colour from the society around us and outside our own patches we keep our heads down. But unlike the Quakers we're not non-violent. If we suffer a wrong we're permitted to fight." For a moment the earlier manner returned. "Were you thinking of going up to the Jebel?"

"I doubt if your people would let me in."

"You are right – they would not. I believe you had a house there once."

"Nothing more than a summer bungalow."

"You will find that it's taken a hit directly. As has other property – whole villages. And more lives lost than a man can think of without rage."

"You mean that American shelling from the sea?"

"Indisputably the crime of the century. Trained infantry can't be stopped by shellfire alone – any senior soldier will tell you that. But a militia can be stopped in its tracks if its families are being murdered behind its back. Yes, it was the crime of the century and moreover it was politically stupid. We were coming down from the hills to join the Shias. We don't love Shias and vice versa but in hatred of foreigners there's nothing between us. If we'd been allowed to make effective contact we might have ended the civil war in a week. But that wasn't what the Americans wanted; they were backing the old establishment. People like you. All they did was to interfere ineffectively."

"Politically they're dangerously innocent."

"I don't mind innocence. I do hate murder." The blue eyes focussed on Khoury squarely; they held a look of what was almost puzzlement. "Isn't that enough to turn you?"

115

'Turn', Khoury thought again. That awful word. "I don't see how I could help you," he said.

"America is the basic enemy and I know that you have never been there. But England is its running dog and you know your England better than any of us." He struck the table with an enormous fist. "You would know where it would really hurt."

"I told you that I'm not a terrorist."

"And I repeat that I know that well. I've been connected with terrorism since I could carry a weapon but I've begun to doubt where it's really getting us. We bomb and we murder, we snatch and we highjack, but empires other than the Anglo-American have lived with a good deal worse than that. Perhaps we're at a dead end – I don't know. But I'd like to try something really new, something they couldn't meet by improving techniques."

"May I ask what?"

"In general terms, yes. I was thinking of some enormous indignity, an utter and final humiliation."

Unexpectedly the Pasha stopped for what he was thinking would hardly move Khoury, this Christian, this westernised man on a tightrope. All Arabs had a legitimate grudge against the West. Of all the races which that West had enslaved none had been treated with quite the contempt it had openly shown for unhappy Arabs. India had had martial races which the British recruited and mostly admired. Even in Africa there were Zulus and Hausa. These men could fight and that was sufficient. An ancient and subtle culture didn't count.

The Pasha rose to his feet at last. "Perhaps even the little I have been telling is too much. So since you're not my man that must end it." He scribbled on a piece of paper. "But if you should ever change your mind ring that number and you'll be brought here discreetly. Do not try to track it down and if you give it to another you're dead." He held out his huge hand politely. "I do

116

not suppose we shall meet again, so good day to you, Mr Adam Khoury. Meanwhile you will be escorted home in a style which befits an ex-ambassador."

One thousand one hundred and sixty miles to the west Willy Smith was reading a message in Queen Anne's Gate. John Paget was too good a stringer to allow excitement to reflect in a communication but Willy caught a whiff of it as he read the words a second time. Paget had had Lord George's instructions and Khoury had been tailed since his landing. Interestingly, the tail had himself been tailed. Khoury had left his home to go shopping and within minutes had been competently kidnapped. Any one of nearly a dozen factions could have done this for one of the usual motives, and he'd been taken across the No-Go Line. But within an hour he'd been brought back unharmed. He was now in his home and observation would continue.

Interesting indeed, Willy thought, but he didn't send a message back. For one thing no new instructions were called for and for another it would be an unnecessary risk. John Paget had a first-class machine but the ease with which he could get information in a country which had fallen to pieces was matched by proportionate risks in getting it out. Communication was complex and often insecure. Willy, who was properly cautious, wouldn't load the frail line with a routine acknowledgement.

On Willy's desk were several telephones and one of them rang now unexpectedly. It was the ordinary public service telephone and it wasn't very often used. Willy picked it up indifferently and a voice told him it had a personal call for him . . . From where? From Belgium.

He would certainly take it. He had only one personal contact in Belgium and that was Mr Stephen Palairet. There was a click as the circuit completed, then:

117

"Good morning, Willy."

"A very good morning." He had recognised the voice at once.

"I take it this line is open?"

"Yes. But it's checked twice daily for any possible tap."

"Then you'll accept the risk?"

"You wouldn't have called if it weren't important."

"At the lowest I think you will find it interesting." A collected pause while the words fell in order. "When we recently met we talked about money. You mentioned a man called Adam Khoury who you suspected had earned a large sum of money from a very suspect source indeed. Hot money which he would have to hide. I explained the system in Belgium for doing so. You remember?"

"I remember the essential, I think. The money would be safe enough in the sense that it would now be laundered but the price was that the holder could welsh with it."

"I couldn't have put it better myself. Then I denied all knowledge of Khoury's affairs, but if he was using the local system I mentioned the name of a major operator whom it was possible he had chosen to hold his loot."

"I remember that too. It was van der Louw. And there were rumours about Menheer van der Louw."

"The reason I am ringing you."

"You mean that he has disappeared?"

"Not at all. He didn't need to disappear – any money he held was formally his. But he has defaulted on his obligations."

"So what happens now?"

"The big row I spoke of. Genuine bankers loathed van der Louw and the government is angry and scared. There was a lot of that sort of money held and of course it's leaving the country in a flood. More important, new money will not come in. But the government can do nothing effective if van der Louw chooses to face it out."

"What does it mean to the wretched depositors? Khoury, for instance. *If* Khoury was one."

"If Khoury rings Menheer van der Louw he will get a polite but recorded answer. It will say that Menheer van der Louw has no record of the caller's business. If everything which Khoury had was hidden away with van der Louw Adam Khoury is at this moment penniless. I just thought I'd let you know."

"I'm grateful."

Willy put down the telephone thoughtfully. There was nothing he could do nor wished to but this information had lit a fuse. He shared Professor Milo's opinion that Khoury was an unstable man.

12

Adam Khoury had passed a very bad night. He recognised the room at once for it had previously held one of the living-in maids. Now there were Uncle George and his son; also a bed and a two-tiered bunk. The boy had politely offered the lower but Uncle George had stuck to the bed without a word. Nor would Khoury have accepted it: the sheets weren't those for a fastidious man. George had snored all night like the pig Khoury thought him and in the morning he had farted malodourously.

Khoury had lain all night on his blanket, sweating in the fanless room, and at five o'clock went to the servants' bathroom. The bath had not been cleaned for a week and though the lavatory worked it made him shudder. There was only cold water but he managed a shave. He then went back to his room and dressed. George had farted again and Khoury opened the window. The morning chill woke Uncle George and he curtly told Khoury to shut it again. Khoury said: "Shut it yourself," and went downstairs.

The household wasn't stirring yet and he went through the hall to the back verandah, sitting in a cane chair and smoking. The garden was a total ruin but that was the last of Khoury's priorities. First he was going to get that bed and clean sheets if he had to go out and buy them. Later, when he had things in hand, he'd get a room to himself if it were physically possible.

The whole *ménage* needed reorganisation and as provider he'd have the right to do it. The two or three men who still had work, who brought in what the others lived on, would be excused any form of domestic labour, but each of the others must have a duty, clearly defined and properly executed. Uncle George, for instance, would clean the baths and the lavatories. He was a peasant and was used to dirt.

That wouldn't be hard but Mama would be difficult. He didn't wish to offend his mother since, offended, she could turn sourly nasty. She thought of herself as a materfamilias but in fact was an inefficient housekeeper. To give her money would be a futile waste. Yes, Mama was going to need careful handling. And if he didn't establish supremacy quickly she would try to marry him off to some cousin. He would keep these people since keep them he must but he wasn't prepared to let them absorb him.

Behind him he could hear the house moving and presently somebody beat a gong. In this broken-down shambles its tone was ironic. He rose and walked back across the squalid hall. In it a dog had left its faeces and Khoury stepped around it in distaste.

The dining room was uncomfortably crowded. There was plenty of the local bread and just enough jam to provide a scraping. No butter and the coffee was bitter, not quite acorns yet but the coarsest Kenyan. He had noticed a woman rather tidier than most of them and he took the empty chair beside her. He introduced himself and waited politely.

"So you're cousin Adam.".

"I suppose I am." He wasn't over-keen to admit it.

"I'm Matilda."

"Mama mentioned you when I saw her yesterday. Apparently you do the shopping."

"I do if you can call it that. I'm lucky that my man's still working but what he and the others bring home isn't much." She looked at what was left of the breakfast, managing a laugh though the sound wasn't joyful. "My apologies for a terrible meal."

121

Adam Khoury had started to like Matilda. She was clean and she spoke respectable Arabic; she was frank and she was clearly competent.

"I intend to make it a little easier."

"For whom?" she asked.

"For you, of course."

She turned honest but shrewd eyes on him thoughtfully. "Thank you very much," she said.

She rose and he rose with her, bowing. For the first time since he'd arrived in this pigsty he was feeling almost pleased with himself. An alliance had been struck without words and in the family in-fighting which he foresaw as inevitable that was something to be prized above rubies.

In the hall the dog's dropping had not been removed but Khoury passed it with almost a smile.

Another little job for Uncle George.

Something else in the hall caught his eye and he picked it up. It was a letter which was addressed to himself and on the back it bore the President's seal. He took it to the verandah and opened it.

At once disappointment and anger fought furiously. For this letter was not from the prisoner President but from the senior of his private Secretaries. Mr Khoury was asked to understand that the President was exceptionally busy and must beg to be excused the formalities. However, an appointment had been made with the head of the Foreign Office. If Mr Khoury would be so good as to telephone an interview would be arranged at his convenience. The letter ended in the customary formula . . . I avail myself of this opportunity. Et cetera.

It was a rebuff and Adam Khoury realised it. Audiences of the President were *de rigueur* for a returning ambassador but he couldn't yet tell how severe the snub was. The President was totally powerless but he was a talkative man and might have let something slip. And that was what Khoury had hoped for – hard news. He

122

telephoned his Foreign Office and made an appointment for half past eleven.

Hard news, he reflected, as he walked along briskly – hard news he must have to make his plans. The Pasha had said he had very good sources and Khoury had entirely believed him. It had therefore been at the least alarming to be told that the British too were having him followed. But he had more than half persuaded himself that this didn't in itself mean a lot. They would strongly suspect, though they couldn't prove, that it was he who had arranged Petra's murder; and they would make a good guess where his fee had come from. Any servant of a man the West feared would be well worth a check on his future movements. In any country, at any time. But Khoury hadn't the least intention of working for the Maghrebi again. He still had most of the Maghrebi's down payment.

Which reminded him: he must check at once. He was going to need that money urgently.

So far he had reassured himself but beyond that lay a real uncertainty. If the British were thinking as the Pasha believed they were they wouldn't be kind to Adam Khoury. They were no longer a world power and accepted it but they still had enough of that useful commodity to make things very hard for an enemy.

That is, if they had decided to do so. That he was going to find out this morning.

He was ushered into the head man's anteroom and kept waiting for a full twenty minutes. Khoury knew that this was a very bad omen. A Presidential snub was one thing but to be kept waiting by his own Head of Service was more serious since it could only be calculated. At last he was shown in and seated.

In England the man who now received him would have carried the resounding tag of Permanent Under Secretary of State. Here he ranked as a *Chef de Cabinet*. And he wasn't the man whom Khoury had expected.

123

From his name as he had introduced himself this man would be a Sunni bigwig and therefore part of the old ruling alliance. That wasn't too bad, they'd have class in common, but Khoury hadn't been told of the change and that began to verge on the sinister.

The *Chef* began on his expected spiel . . . Adam Khoury had been very unlucky indeed. His country's embassies were being downgraded everywhere – plain lack of money made that inevitable – and the only two which were being maintained in anything like their former glory were held by men well senior to himself. Moreover, the men who held Washington and Paris had several years of tenure to run. So Mr Khoury must really see how things stood. The *Chef* spread his hands in a very French gesture. Like most well-to-do Sunnis he had been educated in Paris and privately had little opinion of Khoury's provincial school near London.

Adam Khoury had expected this lecture: these were facts and he had no means to escape them. But he had noticed something else which worried him. He wasn't being thanked for past services. The President had made excuses and this *Chef* had withheld the usual compliments.

Bad again.

Khoury could see that he would have to make a lead. He said that he understood the circumstances and presumed that he'd have to drop at least one grade.

The *Chef* shook his head at once emphatically. A man who'd been an Ambassador could not be taken back in some lesser post. The Service (a very capital S) must recruit the sort of people it wanted and these wouldn't come in if promotion were blocked by a layer of senior officers re-employed.

Adam Khoury knew that this wasn't true; he felt affronted by being put off by that one. There was something behind this charade which he must know. He said deliberately:

124

"What about Hussain Ali, then?"

Hussain Ali had been Ambassador to one of the Scandinavian states. His embassy had been closed like Khoury's but he was working now as a Counsellor in the still considerable establishment in Washington. It was a demotion but he was still in employment.

The *Chef* was feeling affronted too for he disliked being called a liar to his face; but the instinct of an experienced official was to give nothing away unless obliged to. He appeared to consider and then said urbanely:

"The exception which proves the general rule."

Adam Khoury said nothing but laughed insultingly. He was needling this self-satisfied *Chef* and he could see that he had begun to succeed. For his race the *Chef* had an exceptionally fair skin and under it a deep flush was spreading. But for the moment discipline held. He said:

"I'm entitled to resent your attitude."

"I'm entitled to resent prevarication."

It was sufficient to break a lifetime's training; the *Chef* leant forward. "Hussain Ali had an unblemished record."

. . . So the British were doing more than just following him. That would be that man Lord George. It was known that he had contacts everywhere, a network of you-scratch-my-back-I'll-scratch-yours. Lord George had complained and the complaint had been heard. How sympathetically it had been heard he must find out.

"And my pension?" he enquired.

"Not for me – the Treasury." The *Chef* had recovered his earlier urbanity. "Pensions are calculated on the number of years served in the most senior post held." This Adam Khoury knew. "You were unlucky that you only had two in Grade One. In addition I have heard a rumour that there's been some, well, some irregularity. I'm afraid you may have to wait some time and even then you may be disappointed."

So the British were really after him now. Damn them, damn them, damn them to hell.

The *Chef* rose in dismissal and held out his hand. Adam Khoury did not take it.

He walked back to his house thinking hard and fast. He hadn't seriously expected re-employment but he'd expected the full pension he'd earned and perhaps some capital sum for severance. It wouldn't have kept him in brandy and hand-made shoes but it would have been an acknowledgement that he wasn't disgraced. He told himself that it didn't matter. His full pension, if they'd chosen to give it him, a few thousand pounds in compensation, would have been chicken feed against what van der Louw held for him. He must check that at once and make plans accordingly.

The lines from his country to western Europe were uncertain and heavily overloaded but surprisingly he got through at once. A woman answered first and asked him to wait, then a metallic voice came on, a recording.

Menheer van der Louw presented his compliments but had no record of the person calling.

It took nearly a minute of numbness before Khoury felt sick. He pulled himself together shakily and went up to his room where he lay on his bunk. Uncle George's bed had for once been made and Khoury gave it a casual glance. He coveted it no longer now since he couldn't stay in this house to make use of it. They could cut down his pension all right – he knew how. They'd accuse him of some fiddle with his *frais*, insist that the loss be paid from his pension. In fact there had been no such fiddle: on the contrary when he had still had money he had supplemented his *frais* from his private means. But he hadn't a hope of proving that. He shrugged for that was now unimportant. Even if they had paid him in full he couldn't have stayed in this house a day longer, not as one of the two or three others whose pittances kept it just afloat. He had to be the *patron* or nothing.

He thought briefly of Willy Smith but put him aside.

Willy wasn't of consequence now for much more powerful men than Willy had decided to pursue and to break him. In any case Willy Smith was English and his increasing loathing of all things English had been swallowed in a wider hatred, a hatred of the West which had broken him. For Belgium was a Western country, as Western in its way as America. Van der Louw had been a Western man and he'd robbed him like any American con man.

He packed his bags quickly and slipped out of the house, finding a room in a modest lodging house. There he used the telephone, ringing the number the Pasha had given him.

A man's voice answered and asked his business.

He wanted a second interview with a man he'd already met once before.

To his surprise there were no further questions. The voice had sounded entirely incurious. "I'll ring you back in half an hour."

He had a bottle of brandy in one of his bags. He had always kept it carefully locked for he hadn't trusted George an inch. Now he opened it and poured a drink. It was a small one and he drank it slowly. For one thing if the Pasha received him he mustn't appear to be less than stone sober; and for another it was Cypriot brandy and inevitably extremely nasty. The spirit settled his stomach but fuelled his rage.

The telephone rang and he went to it quickly. A voice asked where he was.

Khoury told it.

"Be outside at six. Alone."

Khoury went back to his very small brandy. He wasn't feeling like a Muslim martyr, simply a man who had nothing to live for. But by God! he'd go out with a notable bang.

13

It was a different car but the same two men, both behaving with a formal correctitude. One opened the door of the car and the other said: "I'm afraid it must be the hood again."

"So long as I can breathe a bit."

On the previous journey Khoury had been distinctly uncomfortable. The hood had been heavy where it fell on his shoulders and to the frightening feeling of claustrophobia had been added the fact that he'd had to struggle to breathe.

"I noticed that you were in trouble last time so I've cut a slit for your mouth. Keep your head down, play no games, and you'll be all right."

There was the same devious route to the Line and the halt at it, the same exchange of passwords before they crossed. Then the crawl along the shell-pitted road and the final stop at the Pasha's house. They all got down and Khoury blinked again. The half servant, half sentry was still there with his weapon. Nothing whatever had changed but Khoury.

The Pasha received him standing and smiling. "Delighted," he said. "I'm really delighted. I didn't expect to see you again." His voice came out of his barrel chest with the resonance of a cathedral organ. He wasn't a man to waste time and asked: "What brings you here?"

Adam Khoury told him. He did so crisply for he had considered his words. The Pasha would want facts, not emotions. Those would be sufficiently evident from the fact that he had returned at all. The recital took perhaps ten minutes and at the end of it the Pasha spoke.

"Excellent. Precise and lucid. Most diplomats would have taken half an hour."

Khoury could see he'd acquired much merit. "I've come to you with changed ideas."

"I'm neither blind nor quite insensitive."

"You mentioned a plan . . ." Khoury let it fade.

The Pasha rose and walked to the window. He was looking at the wreck of his garden but he wasn't seeing the tares which now covered it. Gardening wasn't one of his hobbies. In fact he had no hobbies of any kind. Terrorism was his obsession, his life. It filled it every bit as fully as religion filled a dedicated priest's.

He returned from the window and spoke reflectively. "You asked me once if I'd ever employ a Christian. I said I would. Provided he had a sufficient motive. Which you now have and it's called revenge. It isn't a very creditable motive and nothing like the faith which drives me. But while it lasts it's sufficiently powerful." He smiled his surprisingly gentle smile. "To me revenge is quite acceptable."

For the moment, he was secretly thinking, but the moment was all he was going to need.

"Then tell me—"

"I will. But first there is a difficulty. For you, I mean, so I ought to warn you. If I tell you my plan and you turn it down you will have to disappear for some time. Of course as my guest, and you'll be reasonably comfortable but I cannot put a limit on your stay. It may take months or even years to find a man who can offer what you can."

"I'll accept the risk," Adam Khoury said. He would have to; he had no other future.

The Pasha spoke for twenty minutes but as succinctly as Khoury himself. At the end Adam Khoury said simply: "Brilliant."

There was another flash of irritation. Behind the

129

Pasha's courtly manner could be something very ugly indeed. The ordinary rules would mean nothing whatever. Perhaps he was wide open to flattery but not when it was laid on with a trowel. "Nonsense," he said. "An exaggeration. Any competent terrorist could arrange something similar. It's the slant which is original. Which is why I need you."

"Three men to handle the details, I think you said."

"The German will handle the organisation – they're uniformly good at that. In any practical matter you accept his instructions. I think you will get on well with the German since he has much the same background as your own. The Palestinian is the straightforward terrorist. He thinks of killing as a sort of sacrament so you'd do well to keep him sweet if you can. The Japanese is the essential technician. Without his transmitter there's no new slant."

"I follow that. And you have it all covered?"

"The Old Rectory village fête at Wykeham is fixed for Thursday from midday onwards. Ideally you should be dropped in that morning but that needs organisation and we haven't the time. So you'll have to go in at once and hide. I told you I had very good resources and I also have good friends in England. They live in the town where you murdered Petra. Or perhaps you prefer to forget about Petra."

"I very much prefer."

"Then I'll go on. Your three colleagues will leave at once and separately. None of them will be carrying arms – why run a risk at an airport unnecessarily? They won't need anything fancy like rockets, just small arms. My friends are part of a different network, one which the British don't even suspect, and they'll find small arms if I ask them to do so. That essential transmitter goes in with the Japanese. It's of Japanese make and he speaks excellent English. He'll take it in as a commercial sample. No trouble at all." The Pasha waved a hand.

"You think of everything," Khoury said. This time it was admiration, not flattery.

"Which is why I am what I am: a broker. Terrorists come to me with ideas and money. In this case the idea was banal – to snatch a Prime Minister's wife and hold her. If I remember rightly I also told you that I thought that sort of thing was turning sour. Counter-techniques have changed considerably, from the deliberately prolonged exchanges, designed to weaken will, which they do, to the final assault by the SAS. So I gave my client's idea a twist."

"It's a good one," Khoury said. "Very good."

"It's as good as the way you yourself exploit it. Which leads to the question of how you get there. The other three are fairly straightforward. It will be noticed they're not at their usual haunts and this city being the spies' nest it is that news will filter back to the British. In time. In time and they may not be all that interested. But you are under surveillance already. The moment you try to leave this country that fact will be sent back to England."

"May I ask how you've dealt with that?"

"Imperfectly. I have no secret airstrip to spirit you out from so you'll have to use the means by which you came. You'll be followed up to the minute you board and quite possibly on the aircraft itself. But only to your landing in Athens. That is something I can guarantee. Any tail will not get further than Athens."

"And what do I do at Athens airport?"

"You muddy your trail as best you can. Of course it will be unravelled quite easily but that will take a little time. And time is of the essence here. I don't want you at risk in England before two o'clock on Thursday next. So I suggest you buy a ticket to Berne – Berne is notoriously wide open. And from there you buy another to England."

"Where I hide with the others?"

"Certainly not." The Pasha had spoken with proper

131

emphasis but had successfully hidden his private emotion. Which was basically one of envy. This man was almost pitiably innocent but he had expertise which he himself had not. If only he had understood England; if only those Greek police hadn't left him impotent. If only . . .

He would have gone himself.

He recovered and went on explaining smoothly. "For one thing you haven't been trained to hide. Contrary to vulgar opinion it isn't a thing you do quite passively. And for another you might not get on with a colleague. The Palestinian is an animal and you're not the sort of Arab he admires."

"Then where do I go?"

"I'm going to surprise you."

"Very well, surprise me."

"You go to your club."

The prophecy of surprise was amply fulfilled. Khoury repeated blankly: "My club?"

The Pasha said with a hint of mischief: "I heard a little story once though I'm not saying I believe it literally. A police raid caught a fence with some stolen pearls. He hid them by hanging them round his wife's neck. As I say, I think it's a pretty tall story but it makes the essential point, I think. The last place the police will look for you is your club."

"But I know a hundred people there."

"Then do not be seen by a hundred people. You have only two nights to spend there at most – maybe one if you have to wait for your flights. Arrive late at night and go straight to your room. Get up early and go out. Don't eat there. Of course I realise you'll have to eat somewhere but I'd rather you didn't do it in London."

"And how do I get to Wykeham?"

"Openly. Hire a car and arrive at two o'clock. Buy a ticket for the fête and go in. The other three have had

132

their orders so if you hear firing do not get caught in it. When it's over you go to the house and announce yourself. Thereafter you're the political boss, the beautiful political boss. By God! how I wish I could do it myself."

Unexpectedly the Pasha rose again, pacing the room with his bull's head down. His deep voice had risen into a strangled rant; a faint foam flecked his lips as he raved. Sometimes what he said was inaudible and sometimes it came across like a bell. He seemed to be in a sort of ecstasy.

"Think of it, man. Just think of it and praise your God. A thousand insults to the Arab world acquitted in a matter of hours. No demands for vulgar money, not one. No demand to release some brother from prison. Just a calculated act of contempt. They'll have no technique to cope with that. And all of it going out on the air. No secrecy, no possible fudging. You must spin that out for at least two days. Other Western countries sympathising but laughing their smug heads off in private. The indignity, the humiliation! And finally the Prime Minister's woman, pleading, weeping . . . The final act of insult and that's broadcast too."

Khoury could see that the spasm was passing but he didn't try to end it by speaking himself. He was glad of a little time to think for there was one thing he hadn't told the Pasha, something he didn't intend to tell him. He had met Mrs Sara Saint John already and only a fool would predict what she'd do.

The Pasha returned to his desk and normality. His Pashaship might in fact be imaginary but he had one of a gentleman's instincts and said: "I apologise. An exhibition. And your good manners shame my own. Obviously you are going to need money and you haven't mentioned the subject once." He felt in a drawer and produced an envelope. "Two thousand pounds," he said, "in sterling. That should see you through till the end of this mission and after that you won't need money."

"How do you see it ending?"

A shrug. "I said I think they'll talk for at least two days, three if you are really clever. Time to squeeze the lemon dry, the fruit of their humiliation. But at some point they'll have to act and they will. They'll put in the SAS – there'll be shooting. Both ways. In it you will probably die or you may consider the course I would choose myself. But if they take you you'll spend long years in a British jail. Do not be too alarmed at that. Except for chronic overcrowding I hear that they are almost comfortable. By our standards or those of any African state." His smile was one which Khoury couldn't read. "In British penological circles the word punishment is almost unknown. Degeneracy has more than one side to it."

The Pasha changed gear with surprising suddenness. "That Greek shuttle flies twice a day both ways. The first flight tomorrow for Athens is at ten. Go back to your lodging and rest. Pack your bags. You'll be called for at eight o'clock precisely." He rose with an air of completed business. At the door as he shook hands he said:

"It's a pity we shan't get the Prime Minister too. That would be grand slam doubled and vulnerable."

"I'll happily settle to make the small."

Khoury had passed an indifferent night for he had woken twice and each time sweating. With apprehension, he had realised – even fear. But he was committed now; he had no choice. He was privy and he'd accepted eagerly. The man who had accepted was no longer a half westernised diplomatist, but quintessentially a vengeful Arab.

The car called at eight o'clock to the minute with the same two men but this time in uniform. They wore baggy and rather dirty fatigues but their boots were clean. Both of them were armed, now openly. One had an Uzi ("We owe the Israelis thanks for those,") and the other what Khoury thought was a Steyr.

They took a different route to the broken airport from that which the taxi had used in arriving, closer to the Camps and their miseries. Several times they were stopped by pickets but each time they were allowed to pass. The car came at length to the waiting aircraft where their arms exacted immediate space, for Khoury and his modest suitcases. Otherwise it was the same grim horror, the press of bodies and the nagging fear. How many more trips could this deathtrap make before it fell into the sea in pieces? Khoury noticed that the pilot was different so perhaps other men had wondered too. He had expected that some animal instinct would warn him if he were being followed but such a sense, if he had ever had it, had atrophied over his years of ease. There was a single other European so as likely as not it might be he. Khoury thought so but he didn't feel it.

At Athens he cleared and walked to another desk, buying a ticket for Berne in cash. It was extraordinarily simple and even casual. He wasn't even asked for his passport.

He had three hours to wait and had had no breakfast. There would be a meal on the aircraft but that would be terrible, stale meats and salads in plastic wrappings. He saw that the bar sold coffee and croissants and he went to it and ordered greedily. Neither would be very good but compared to what he'd been eating they'd be superb.

He was well into his second helping when he heard a cry behind him, then uproar, the sound of men running fast in a body and the characteristic frenetic babble which only Greeks in panic could contrive. He turned on his stool but the barman said sharply:

"Don't do that. Don't get involved. The police can hold you as a material witness for as long as they please and that's for months."

A man slid onto the stool beside him. He was a

Frenchman but he spoke first in English. "Just another bloody Arab vendetta. Man with a knife in his heart, struck upwards. Left to right so it misses the ribcase. Professional. I've seen it before."

"He wasn't a European?"

"Why should he be a European?"

"I was wondering—"

"An extremely foolish thing to do. *Faisons semblants de ne pas l'avoir vu*." He spoke to the barman in some incomprehensible patois. "If the police come over the barman will vouch for us. We've been sitting here for half an hour. May I offer a drink?"

"A brandy, please."

"I'll have the same." He paid for them with a twenty pound note. He hadn't seemed to expect any change.

Adam Khoury was feeling reassured. The Pasha had said he might be shadowed but that if he were it would end at Athens. As it had. This mission might be entirely unorthodox, something never attempted before, but he was evidently in experienced hands.

14

John Paget had been obliged to make an awkward decision but he was a senior operator who was allowed some discretion. Further, he could trust his masters. They wouldn't savage him if he had made a mistake. He had left his post without permission.

This unheard of desertion had been dictated by urgency: his news was red hot but his communications were slow. He wasn't the sort of theatrical operator who was dropped on a sensitive spot with a radio, hoping to get a message back before he was inevitably caught. In this city which had been Khoury's birthplace nothing was secret but little counted as hard news. There'd been ample time to filter the rumours and to send back the pieces that mattered at leisure. That had meant using the British embassy. As an auxiliary in the one hospital working Paget had a regular contact for one of the staff came in weekly for treatment. But he had been in only the day before and Paget couldn't wait another week.

It was a difficult decision but he took it. He slipped across a land frontier quietly, took a taxi to the capital and thence the first flight which was leaving for London. Anything he owned of value he could carry in a single suitcase but the furniture of his flat he left behind. He wasn't too greatly troubled by that for the Executive could be notably generous. Its resources weren't subject to Treasury audit. It was more serious that he had blown for ever a cover which had been built up over the years. The Executive wouldn't like that at all but he believed they would consider it justified.

He was with them now in Queen Anne's Gate, not sitting before the Board in line like some candidate at a *viva voce* but at ease at a round table, an equal. The whole Board was present, taut as drums, and the Prime Minister was taking the meeting. He had won an election by facing the unpopular and in a crisis his other virtues were evident. He tapped a paper on the table before him, then turned to John Paget. "We've all read this and it's admirably condensed. Now tell it as it happened, please."

"Start at the beginning?"

"That's always best."

"Then my instructions were to shadow Khoury. He was taken across the Line and I thought he'd been snatched. When he came back the same day I was puzzled."

"Naturally," the Prime Minister said. "And the next sighting of any significance was when?"

"Was next day when he paid a call at his Foreign Office. I'm told that he came out looking furious. Obviously I don't know why."

Lord George interrupted. "But I can guess."

"Do so," the Prime Minister said.

"He'd been given a rocket and not re-employed."

"You didn't tell me that before."

"I didn't think you'd be very much interested." Lord George was as urbane as a Jesuit. "I knew that you didn't much care for diplomats, particularly one who is also a murderer."

The Prime Minister could have asked several questions but Lord George had an effective network, the ability to give *quid pro quo*, and whatever he had done was in the past. He returned to Paget. "Please go on."

"Then he moves out to a boarding house but next morning he's called for, peacefully this time, and taken across the Line as before. As you know, we cannot follow him there but we picked him up again at the airport. We

138

even had a man on his flight but he didn't get further than Athens. Where he was knifed."

"So when Khoury crossed the Line – the second time, voluntarily – he was contacting somebody pretty powerful?"

John Paget had a fastidious mind. "I don't think we can call that deduction but it's something I would certainly bet on."

"A big-shot terrorist?"

"Yes, I think so."

"Khoury contacting a big-shot terrorist?" It sounded more surprised than doubting. Clement Saint John looked at Milo. "Your turn."

"I'm as surprised as you are but not incredulous. Adam Khoury was a complex man and we know he'd been under increasing pressure. A private crisis might tip his uneasy balance."

The Prime Minister glanced at the paper before him. "And these other three men?"

"That's hearsay, sir." John Paget had been a regular soldier and 'sir' was his inherited language. He disapproved of the civil service habit of calling a senior officer 'Minister'. "It didn't come to me through my own men, you see. But that city is a sounding board and three experienced terrorists have left their usual haunts."

The Commissioner said: "Permission to speak?" He had noticed Paget's 'sir' and liked it. He too had been a regular soldier.

"Of course you have. Go on."

"We've had an hour or two for the usual hack-work, and though the airport at Athens is in the usual Greek chaos we've discovered that Khoury booked on for Berne. Berne is being unhelpful on principle but a man is on his way there by air. Meanwhile we're assuming that Khoury's target is England."

"Will he get in here?"

"With any luck, yes. The airports have been warned,

of course, but if he's working for whom I'd guess he is he'll have a different and a very good passport. We've already sent out a description and photograph but my hunch is that he's here already."

"And the other three men?" the Prime Minister asked.

Jack Pallant waved a hand at Paget. "Your end again," he said. "How much do we know?"

"According to our information, and I emphasise that it isn't direct, one speaks nearly perfect English and the other two can speak enough. Their papers will be in apple-pie order and I'd guess they'll come in as commercial travellers. Separately, almost for certain."

"When they'll all join up and go into hiding?"

It was Lord George who answered the question. "No. On form, as it's known, that's rather improbable. The three may hide together but not with Khoury. Hundreds of people in England know him. The risk would be disproportionate to anything which could be conceivably gained. So Khoury will make his own arrangements and I'd guess they would be something unusual. And they won't join up till the day of whatever they plan."

The Commissioner came in at once. "Of course we've put the dragnet on but they're needles in the proverbial haystack."

"I do not expect what I know is impossible." The Prime Minister had intended to sound emollient but his voice had retained the edge it had started with. He repeated what Lord George had just said. " 'They won't join up till the day of whatever they plan.' So we'd better look at the major targets." He turned his head back to the most senior of all policemen.

Who had expected the question and knew the answers. "The Royals first – we've been lucky there. The major Royals are on that Yacht. A visit to Sweden though God knows why. The minors are an insoluble problem. We can't saturate every house they live in but we'll alert the so-called detectives who guard them. They can shoot though they're not up to Greenjacket standards. You yourself and your wife are also prime targets."

"I'm staying on in London indefinitely."

"Good. And your wife, if I may ask it?"

"She'll be going down to Wykeham quite soon – the annual fête. Lady Bountiful and all that, you know." There was something in the tone which made them stare. The Prime Minister was clearly worried but apparently not for his wife's security. It was a private and very personal trouble. They dropped their eyes.

Jack Pallant said: "There's a drill for that too. When your wife goes down to Wykeham we send two men. They're good ones and they cover her closely."

Unexpectedly the Prime Minister rose. "Then that seems to hold it. As far as we can which is not very far. The target is unknown but it will be big." He gave them his characteristic bow, something between an old-fashioned head waiter's and the brief curt nod of the professional courtier. "Good morning, gentlemen. And thank you."

When he and Paget had gone they relaxed almost visibly. They would have agreed that he'd handled the meeting perfectly but there was something about his terse incisiveness which occasionally came close to abrasion.

Lord George got up and went to the sideboard. He poured sherry for himself and for Pallant. "Milo, I know what you like already." It was gin and tonic and not too much tonic. He also fixed a drink for Willy without even needing to ask what he wanted. At this time of the morning Willy drank soda water.

Over the drinks they relaxed some more. Milo said reflectively: "I found the Prime Minister rather surprising."

"I know he can be a little, well, short."

"I didn't mean that. He seemed privately pleased."

"He was as pleased as a cat with two tails and I'll tell you why. Remember that his wife is my niece so I know

141

him rather better than most men. If he has an obsession it's the world of diplomacy. He meant it when he told us once that if only we could give him the evidence he'd put Khoury on trial and to hell with the protocol. Well, he's only an ex-ambassador now but if we catch him in sin that will flutter the dovecots. Some of their more preposterous inhabitants may even think twice before chancing their arms again. As nowadays they do quite freely. Weapons in diplomatic bags, sanctuary when it isn't justified, even shooting from an embassy window."

Willy as the junior present had so far preserved a seemly silence. "*If* we catch him," he said now.

"Quite so. I agree with what the Prime Minister said himself. 'The target is unknown but it will be big.' This is pretty heavy stuff we're up against: a vengeful man and three high-class terrorists. It won't be some murderous bomb in a shop. But in one thing we've been distinctly lucky. The Prime Minister is staying in London, and in Downing Street and his usual movements we have him pretty well covered as a drill. Long may he remain in London."

"I'll drink to that," Milo said.

"So will I."

At the Security Executive the night-duty officer was picked from the list of senior operators, but influenza had cut this list by a third and Willy, as the most junior Director, had volunteered to stand his turn. It wasn't an exacting job provided there were no active crises; it was even possible to sleep in a chair but Willy Smith wasn't good at that. He twitched and sweated and woke up miserable. And when he got home Amanda would go for him. Not overtly since they seldom quarrelled but she'd let him see that she disapproved of his doing a job which he didn't have to. Like many good wives she was properly sensitive on the subject of her husband's status. Very well, then – the never-failing emollient. He

142

would call at a florist before he went home. The shops would hardly be open yet but there was a market a mile to the west of his house and he'd take very good care to go there first.

The day-duty man came in at seven o'clock. "Anything of interest?" he asked.

"Nothing for us. Some Sikh has taken a pot at Ghandi but it was a home-made gun and he missed by a yard."

"Pity," the duty man said.

"May be."

As Willy passed a mirror he glanced at it, deciding that he looked like a tramp. His clothes betrayed that he had slept in them, which he had. But in his days as an operator Willy had evolved a simple drill for this. You took with you a modest night-bag – razor, clean underwear, shirt and a freshly pressed suit. He collected this now and walked across the park to his club.

The night porter answered his ring and let him in. Willy intended to change in the lavatory. He was provident in small expenses and it would have been extravagant to hire a bedroom simply to shave and change his clothes. He tried the lift but it wasn't yet working so he began to climb the noble staircase.

And halfway up it he froze like the pillar of salt. A man was coming down it fast with a suitcase in each hand, not turning his head. He didn't acknowledge Willy Smith but there was the flash of instant recognition.

The man had been Mr Adam Khoury, ex-ambassador, murderer, now suspect terrorist.

Willy was with Lord George in half an hour.

Who was dressed and drinking his morning coffee. Like Willy he seldom ate English breakfasts and his wife, an Italian who was putting on weight, never ate any breakfast at all. Lord George took a single look at Willy.

"Willy, you look like a walking wounded. Would you rather talk straightaway or clean up first?"

"I think I'd better talk first."

"Very well. Have some coffee."

He poured and Willy drank as he talked. "I thought of stopping him but I didn't have power to. Also he might have been armed and I was not. He looked pretty tense."

"A wise decision. Besides, one doesn't brawl in respectable clubs."

Lord George heard the rest out in total silence, then asked a single question sharply. "The day man has relieved you?"

"Of course."

"Then we'd better check on the VIPs." He took the telephone and gave an order. The telephone operator said: "Ten minutes."

"Make it nine."

It rang back in eight and a half precisely. Lord George told Willy to take the extension.

The major Royals were still on their Yacht and reputedly bored rigid by the Swedes.

And the minors?

. . . Exceptionally quiescent. One Colonel-in-Chief was dining in but her regiment would be duly alerted. The others were mostly staying at home and their detectives would be put on notice.

The Prime Minister hadn't changed his plans?

. . . If he had he hadn't let anyone know.

No gathering of notables?

. . . None. No Lord Mayor's dinner – nothing like that.

Lord George said: "Thank you," and put down the telephone. An intellectual would not have considered him clever for they wouldn't have had a wavelength in common; and an academic might have misread him as dim. In fact he had a lucid mind and it slipped into gear with an almost audible click.

"We decided at that last meeting of ours that those four men wouldn't join up till the day of the strike.

144

Khoury has packed and left his hideout so presumably that day is today."

"If our assumption was right that's perfectly logical."

"But there's no major target and that doesn't fit."

"Then it must be a minor. There are hundreds of those – we can't possibly cover them."

"I think it's worth our while to cover one." Lord George began to lay them down. "Today is the day of the fête at Wykeham and the Prime Minister's wife will be there for certain. And it isn't the ordinary village do – not just home-made jam and cakes and a sideshow. There's a funfair comes in to the paddock and there's a band. Usually it ends up with dancing. It's all advertised in the local resorts and people come in from the coast in coaches. It even makes a good deal of money for the church. My niece may have some unorthodox habits but she's very good at business indeed." He added blandly. "We always were."

"Objection—" Willy began.

"I know it. You could snatch a Prime Minister's wife and hold her – for money perhaps or the release of some prisoner. Something like that has often been done before. *But what's Khoury doing in that sort of set-up?"*

Willy knew no answer but said: "When Mrs Saint John goes down to Wykeham two plainclothes men go with her as routine. It would be easy to send more."

"Easy but I think a mistake. To begin with this is only a guess and the Commissioner will not be pleased if coachloads of his valuable manpower are sent off on a mission which ends in nothing. And secondly there's an objection of principle. I don't want a GMFU at all costs, and premature reinforcement invites one."

"Too often."

"But I would like to know what goes on at the Rectory." Lord George looked at Willy Smith in enquiry. "I know you've had a miserable night but we're unusually short of first-class men. Could you manage it yourself?"

"I'd like to."

"In that case you'll need instructions. Here they are. If anything happens in no circumstances get mixed up in it. No heroics. It's information I want, not a dead Willy Smith. Run for the nearest telephone. I'll stay at the shop till half past six and thereafter you can get me here."

"Any hint of what I'm looking for?"

"None."

"I think I deserve to know what's in your mind."

"Fair enough." Lord George took two turns round the room and sat down again. "I suspect that this isn't a common snatch. That's possible but it's also old hat. Our techniques in kidnaps have changed a lot and a common or garden hold-and-demand hardly calls for three outstanding men, plus a man who was once a Grade One Ambassador. What I fear is something entirely new, some twist which hasn't been used before."

"Lucky the PM won't be there."

"Very lucky indeed. Then good luck, Willy."

"I hope I don't need it."

"So sincerely do I."

An hour later Willy was back with Amanda. She gracefully accepted the flowers for what they were, a burnt offering to a good wife's displeasure. "I see you've had time to change," she said, "but you're looking pretty knackered. Tell."

He knew she was secure and did so.

"A village fête in the country," she said. "I love them."

"Then I'll take you to one sometime."

"No. Today."

He said on a reflex: "I couldn't possibly."

His wife's reaction greatly surprised him; he had expected protest and even anger but instead received a

146

cool dose of reason. "Willy, you're not using your head. They're sending you down to Wykeham as a spy. If anything happens you're not to tangle."

"How did you guess?"

"You're too valuable to lose."

He realised he was being flattered but could recognise good sense when he heard it. And he didn't wish to risk a fuss when she'd let him off the one he'd expected. He said, but on a note of uncertainty:

"To take you would be very irregular."

"You're a very irregular organisation. If you weren't you'd be just a department with numbers."

It was true again and he thought it over. There was no point in fighting a losing battle. She hadn't said it but if he pressed her she would. If he didn't take her she'd go alone. She was set on her day in the country. So be it.

"My orders if anything happens are to run."

"Anything you can do I can do better."

He conceded a game which he couldn't win. If she went alone they could easily get separated. "Then stick to me like a leech all day."

"I'll stick to you like the good wife I am."

Half annoyed but half amused he nodded. "These things don't come alive till the afternoon. We'll have lunch on the way."

Another couple was also talking, the Prime Minister, Clement Saint John, and Sara. He was a man who had never been known to shout but his manner was at its most incisive. "I hear you've asked Milo to Wykeham for the fête."

She nodded but she held her peace. She had recognised that tone at once.

"I don't think you should do that."

"Why not?" It was no good beating the bush with Clement. If she didn't put it in words then he would.

147

"I don't think you can accuse me of stuffiness. I've behaved like some man in a modern novel."

"I don't read modern novels much. Not the sort which wins the Booker."

His laugh was sincere but the bait he declined. "It isn't what you do but the how and the where. Particularly in this case the where." He collected himself and then said crisply: "Not in a man's own house, you don't."

Her surprise was as genuine as her husband's laugh. "Aren't you being a little middle class?"

"You put it very well, my dear. Middle class is what I am. And proud of it."

"But I can't put Milo off."

"I don't ask it. I do ask what day he's coming and when."

She hesitated but he had means to find out. "On Thursday," she said. "For the fête in the afternoon."

"Then I'll be coming down on Thursday morning."

15

Willy and Amanda Smith had driven leisurely and lunched at a pub. They left the A12 at Marks Tey and turned north, into country which was changing fast. Once it had been straight agricultural with the occasional mansion like Lord George's own Wykeham, but mainly modest manors and farmhouses. The farming still existed prosperously, barley and sugarbeet and rape, but the manors and the village houses were no longer held by country gentlemen or the merchants who had served the farmers. They were owned by well-to-do commuters, the sort who could get in at half past nine. A sensitive nose could smell new money. They motored up to twenty miles, then took the fast trains which came from Norwich. Never the others which started at Clacton. On those one met disagreeable people.

Amanda was reading a map efficiently. "Right in a mile for the village," she said. "The other road goes up to the big house."

"Where Lord George's eldest half-brother still lives. In a flat in one wing," Willy added sadly. "The rest is National Trust and you pay to go in. It's something called redistribution of wealth."

"You don't approve?"

"I'm never quite sure. One way or another it had to come but we seem to have got the worst of both worlds." He gave her an enquiring glance. Amanda wasn't politically minded.

"Tell me about the Rectory and the fête."

"Lord George's family once held the advowson and

they gave the living to the Prime Minister's father. He died there and Clement Saint John was born. Later, when the house got too big for any priest without a private income, the Church Commissioners sold it off. There were one or two owners, I don't know who, then the Prime Minister bought it as a weekend retreat. He spent his boyhood there and he married a local so in a sense you could say that he bought it back."

"So happy ending," Amanda said.

"I sometimes wonder."

They had squeezed past a coach going much too fast. Inside it people were singing boozily and children were waving flags from the windows.

"I see what you mean," Amanda said. "And the fête?"

"There's been a Rectory fête at Wykeham for centuries. Now it's a commercialised jolly. No doubt it makes a lot more money – Sara Saint John has seen to that – but for my part I would guess it's been spoilt."

"Not for me."

As they neared the village the traffic thickened, more coaches and cars whose drivers swore crossly. There were police out in force to direct the flow. The car park for the crowded coaches was opposite the Rectory itself but the park for private cars was further on. Perhaps, Willy thought, that was somehow significant.

They walked back along the lane to the little lodge. Normally the housekeeper lived there but today it was being used to sell tickets. A man sat outside at a trestle table and already there was a considerable queue. In fact there was no need to form one since the Rectory and its modest policies, garden, handsome lawn and paddock, were neither fenced nor wired in against entry. It would have been easy to walk in through the fields. Perhaps some people had but not many.

Willy and Amanda bought tickets and went in. The drive curved right to the house itself but a spur went straight on to the garden behind it. There was a signpost which said TO THE FETE in large capitals and behind it a local policeman to reinforce. You might have paid your pound at the lodge but that didn't include the private front garden.

The house itself was clearly visible and, though the uniformed policeman fidgeted, Willy and his wife stopped to look at it, absorbing its indefeasible aura. Originally it had been built in the local materials but later, with many others like it, it had been rendered and painted over in white. There were finely proportioned sash windows, a modest porch. That was the inescapable word: the whole house was modest. Generations of hard-working priests had lived here in the days when the national Church of England had been not only established but part of the country's life.

They turned and walked up the spur to the back of the house. Here the aura of modesty changed dramatically. The crowd was of two recognisable types: the locals in their seemly best and the people from the coastal resorts in casual clothes which were often flashy. There were stalls and a marquee for tea, another which was selling beer. Brewster Sessions, Willy Smith thought cynically, would be indulgent to a Prime Minister's wife. In the paddock the funfair was crowded and noisy. A steam organ was thumping remorselessly. Amanda said: "We'd better do the stalls before we go on."

They went from one to the other indifferently. They bore the humble offerings to their parish church of people who occasionally still used it; jam and cakes and unwanted bric-a-brac. Willy was trying to spot the two plainclothes guards. In this he was unsuccessful but unsurprised. The days were long since gone and forgotten when you could tell a plainclothes copper by his walk. Presently Amanda stopped unexpectedly. "Honey in the comb," she said. "I haven't seen that for years. We must have some."

There was a woman behind the stall looking bored.

Amanda asked her politely: "How much a comb, please?"

The woman told her.

"I'll take four if I may but I'll come back for them later. If that's all right with you, of course. We were going to the funfair, you see, and the last thing anyone wants on a roundabout is four unbroken combs of honey."

The woman was too well bred to show her surprise. In this part of the world West Indians were a rarity and a West Indian speaking her own sort of English unknown. And she liked the look of Willy Smith.

"I'll tell you what I'll do," she said. "I'll take them up to the house and put them in a box for you. When you've finished with the funfair just knock on the door."

"That's really extremely kind. Too kind."

"Not at all. I don't often sell four combs at a time."

Willy could see they were in for a chat but knew no reason they shouldn't have one. The woman asked pleasantly: "Where are you from?"

"We live near Clapham Common," Amanda said.

It wasn't the answer the woman had expected but she recovered quickly and went on. "There are some fine old houses on Clapham Common."

"I suppose you could say we have one ourselves. Actually it's my mother's still but she lives on the top floor and we have the rest. She's seventy-five but as spry as can be."

More than spry enough, Amanda remembered, to bring in the little pot we need.

Sara Saint John was no longer bored. She was entertained and wanted more. "I was thinking of a cup of tea." She caught Amanda's glance at the marquee. "Not there. In the house. I live there."

"We'd love to."

Willy had tapped Amanda's ankle for if anything untoward happened it would happen here outside, not

152

in the house. But she hadn't paid the least attention. Willy Smith sighed. There wasn't a woman he knew or had heard of who could resist the temptation of seeing another's house.

Sara signalled to a second woman who had been hovering in the background discreetly. "Mary, it's coming up for your shift. Be an angel and mind the shop for half an hour."

They walked across the lawn to the terrace and through the French window which led to the living room. The first man Willy saw was Clement Saint John. He got to his feet at once, said:

"Why Willy!"

His wife could be forgiven surprise. "You know each other already?"

"Of course. We sit on the same Board of business." Milo had risen in greeting too. "And so does Milo here, as it happens." He turned to Amanda and bowed politely. "You must be Willy's wife."

"I am."

"I've always badly wanted to meet you."

They all sat down and Sara Saint John poured tea. Willy was in sharp embarrassment for the Prime Minister's presence at Wykeham had shocked him; he was supposed to be sitting safely in Number Ten. Willy's duty was to run to the telephone, to contact Lord George and warn him of bad news. But good manners inhibited that entirely. Moreover if he breached them and did so the Prime Minister would rebuke him sharply. He was known to detest all forms of security – security on his person, that is – considering them both irritating and useless. By instinct and by acquired experience his private beliefs were fatalistic. If the angel of death had marked him he would call.

Willy tried to comfort himself by a knowledge of what in fact would happen. It was possible that the Prime Minister had told nobody of his change of plan but Prime

153

Ministers couldn't just disappear. His absence would be noticed quickly and there was an obvious guess as to where he had gone. Or if he had come on a sudden impulse his driver was trained and would know his duty. He would have telephoned to his headquarters by now.

So within two or three hours there'd be reinforcements, the usual guard for a VIP when he annoyingly wished to visit his own house. Armed men would be arriving in coaches, possibly even a vanguard by helicopter.

That was all right, Willy thought – when it happened. But for the moment Clement Saint John was uncovered. Three front-rank terrorists were at large, plus Khoury, and the Prime Minister of the United Kingdom was guarded by two policemen with handguns.

Willy joined the chatter politely . . . What a very small place the world was, really, and yes, it had been a lovely day. The fête had a reputation for lovely days. And of course it was the funfair which made the real money. It paid a respectable rent and a share of the takings, though Sara suspected that these were fiddled.

As they talked Willy Smith inspected the fine room. He could see that it had once been two, for the Rector's study where he wrote his sermons (or more likely, Willy considered, just cribbed them) had been joined with what he had called the parlour. The existing room ran the length of the house. From the French window where they'd come in you could see the lawn and, looking the other way through the study, the drive and the private garden beyond it.

There was a squeal of brakes and a spatter of gravel as a car pulled up on the well-raked drive. Three men got out and started to run. They ran down the blind side towards the lawn. The Prime Minister said indignantly:

"They've got a nerve."

Willy who'd had a closer view could see that they had

had more than that. Two of them had been carrying weapons.

There was a second of astonished silence, then two single shots from outside on the lawn. Instantly a long burst of automatic fire.

The two men I didn't spot, poor bastards. They wouldn't have had a chance against that.

Three men came in through the open French window. Two of them carried machine pistols confidently and at their muzzles faint curls of acrid smoke fouled the air. The third held what looked like an outsize radio.

A fourth man came in through the window behind them. "Adam Khoury," he said. "You will please behave sensibly."

He gave Sara a smile and nodded briefly to Willy. They froze in a sort of tableau. Turning to the Prime Minister he said: "Mr Clement Saint John, I presume."

"Correctly. May I ask—"

"By all means. The tallest of my friends is a German. He holds a doctorate from your own university. The Japanese speaks excellent English. The third is a Palestinian Arab who can understand English but prefers not to speak it."

"Then allow me to complete the formalities. My wife you appear to know already and Willy Smith I know you do. The lady with him is Mrs Smith and the man on the sofa is Professor Ignatius Milovic." The Prime Minister sounded entirely unruffled. These terrorists might have been his guests and he a good host trying to put them at ease. His wife gave him a glance of approval and something more.

Adam Khoury had returned to the German. "It's for you to make the arrangements."

"Thank you. The women are to be taken upstairs. In the attic are two bedrooms with a connecting door. There is also a bathroom. *En suite*, I rather think they call it."

He's been very well briefed, Willy thought – *very* well. That was something they must follow up later.

If there was a later to follow up in.

"So the women go upstairs as I say. It's too high to jump so they needn't be guarded. In any case we haven't the manpower. Just lock them in. They're to be fed and watered at reasonable intervals but if there's a telephone tear it out. Tomorrow when the air will be full of us you can take them a portable set to amuse them." He turned to the Arab. "Will you do that, please?"

The Arab looked at Sara first; he had noticed her handbag and held out his hand for it. He weighed it reflectively, finally satisfied. It was too light to hold what he considered a weapon and he didn't wish to look inside. His background was puritanical and he wouldn't risk offence from a woman's bag. There'd be cosmetics and pills and very probably worse. All Western women were secretly whores.

He took the two women upstairs at gunpoint.

The German was continuing smoothly. "I'm afraid you men will be rather less comfortable. I mentioned that we were short of manpower so you'll have to stay down here with us. You may sleep as you wish or indeed are able and when we have time for food ourselves we will give you a share of what we find. You may also go to the lavatory on demand but you will not be permitted to wash or shave." For the first time the German allowed a smile. "There's nothing disorientates a Western man more than the knowledge that he is unshaven and dirty."

Milo caught 'disorientates' clearly. It frightened him but he controlled his face. In his profession the word had a very sick meaning.

The German looked at the Japanese who had been busy while the others talked. He had plugged in his set to a convenient power socket and taken the baseplate off the telephone. From it a wire now ran to the big black

156

box. From where he sat Willy Smith saw its face and he didn't think it looked much like a radio. The extensible aerial almost reached to the ceiling and there were switches and dials which domestic radios did not have. On top of the box was a microphone and a loudspeaker.

The German asked: "How's it going?"

"I think well." The Japanese began to explain. "Anything said on the telephone, either way, goes out on the air through the transmitter directly. The rest of us will hear it relayed on that speaker." He pointed. "The same thing the other way, more or less. The microphone picks up anything said in here." He pressed a switch and produced a faint hum. "The circuits seem in perfect order but we can't be sure till the first incoming call."

"Which shouldn't be long." It was Adam Khoury.

The Palestinian swung on him swiftly and savagely. "You're not in charge till it does," he said. He spoke in a harsh unmelodious Arabic.

Milo who lived by observing correctly caught the sudden flare of bitter malice. Well, it was not surprising, that. Khoury was an educated man who had once been rich. For all this Arab knew he might be still. Whereas he himself was a peasant with arms, consumed by a fire which Adam Khoury did not share. Naturally he would hate such a man. Milo didn't think in terms of class: that was something for the *bons penseurs* he despised. He thought in older and more explicit words. They were envy, hatred and all uncharitableness.

The German said peaceably: "Then let's wait for that call."

They did so for maybe an hour, not talking, till the silence was broken by the thud of the helicopters. They flew over the house and landed quickly. "That's only the vanguard but quite soon it will be dark. So we'd better know their dispositions." The German turned to the Arab and added: "Would you go upstairs and see what you can, please?"

157

The Arab left the room with his weapon. It was as much a part of him now as the air he breathed. Milo had noticed the 'please' with disquiet. This man was a killer and moreover enjoyed it.

He came back in ten minutes, reporting curtly. "They've taken over the lodge," he said.

"Good. There's a telephone."

"And I think they have men in the paddock too."

It was a fact. The shooting had cleared it like a charge by mounted police. The steam organ had gone on for five minutes, then expired in a diminishing groan.

"I don't think it matters how they've placed themselves. They're not going to rush us or not yet. They'll give us time and time's our friend."

The telephone rang as the German was speaking. He nodded briefly to Khoury. "All yours from now on. Good luck."

Adam Khoury picked up the telephone. "To whom am I speaking?"

A voice gave a name and the rank of Superintendent. He'd been trained in this work but had little faith in it. Colloquially it was called the Talk Out and the statistics were rather firmly against it. Of nine recent cases two had succeeded but the other seven had ended in shooting. So why not send in the soldiers at once? But he had had his instructions and intended to follow them. He said, as he'd been trained to, affably:

"What can I do for you?"

"Nothing whatever."

It wasn't at all the answer expected. Wisely the Superintendent stayed silent.

"Or rather you can do nothing positive. We have no demands of any kind. On the negative side you will not cut the services, particularly the electricity. If you do there will be instant reprisals."

Cutting off the services was the last step before sending in the men with the guns and the Superintendent said: "Yes," by reflex. "How are you for food?" he asked.

It was Move Two in this ridiculous drill.

"We are perfectly all right for food." Khoury hadn't checked but was sure. A house like this always had food. There'd be a deepfreeze and a stock of tins. Even, if he were lucky, brandy.

"You're sure you have no message for me to pass on? My superiors will be coming soon."

"I told you. We have no demands."

The voice recovered a note of authority. "Two policemen are lying outside on the lawn. I am sending in four men with two stretchers."

"If you do so they will be shot."

"What was that?"

"I think you heard me perfectly clearly."

"But one or both may still be alive."

"Hold the line, please." Khoury turned to the Palestinian. "They're worried that one of those policemen may still be alive."

The Arab got up and went outside. Presently there was a single shot. He returned, put a thumb up and sat down again quietly.

"Are you there still?"

"I am. I heard a shot—"

"One man was already dead."

The Superintendent said softly: "Jesus Christ."

"If your friends were Christians they're doubtless with Him."

The voice changed to utter outrage. "It's shameful."

"My own word would not be shameful but shaming." Khoury looked at the Japanese in enquiry.

It would have been bad manners to show that he felt triumphant but it was permissible to show satisfaction. "All that went out on the air as spoken. Every ham within fifty miles will have picked it up. Every national daily will have it in headlines tomorrow."

159

16

The Cabinet was in emergency session and Lord George and the Commissioner had been bidden to attend and advise. Since Lord George had once been Foreign Secretary and was therefore a Privy Councillor his appearance would not have shocked a traditionalist, but no precedent covered the presence of Sir Jack. This was a crisis and was being dealt with *ad hoc*.

The Home Secretary was the acting Chairman for he was Deputy Prime Minister. That shadowy office he filled to perfection since he was a shadowy man himself with blurred edges. He was an excellent Home Secretary since his instincts were to fudge and to compromise, attributes which were admirably suited to an office which was itself a balancing act; but he had none of Clement Saint John's incisiveness, none of the Prime Minister's zest in meeting a crisis head on and beating it. Behind his back he was called the Weasel.

He tapped on the table but without authority. Like one of those Staff College Brigadiers, Pallant thought, commanding three tough Lieutenant Colonels all of whom had seen more fighting than he had. 'Orders' would not be orders at all but a basis for free discussion and comment. The DPM said: "Gentlemen," and slid his eye round the crowded table. It stopped at the Minister of Posts and Telegraphs. "The basic problem is of course that transmitter. What is your advice on that?"

It had been characteristic of Clement Saint John that he had appointed to that dreary Department a man with some knowledge of electronics. He didn't say: "I am told," or "I understand,"; he answered from personal knowledge, crisply. "We daren't cut the current since they've threatened reprisals but after that it depends what they've got there. They're not trying for long-distance transmission but in the area which they cover they're strong. I can guess what you're thinking – why not mush them? We could do that if they stuck to one wavelength but already they've switched twice and may switch again. They're not sending to the domestic listener but to the hams who can pick them up quite easily, the people who stay up all night to get Reykjavik. Plenty can do that and more and by now the newspapers will be listening directly. You have to take it from me we can't jam them."

The DPM nodded in reluctant acceptance. "What I don't understand is these people's motive."

For answer somebody held up a newspaper. It wasn't one of the more intellectual but sold widely and to a varied public. Its banner headline read simply: SHAME.

The Foreign Secretary saw it and cut in crossly. "And it isn't only the papers," he said. "The French ambassador rang this morning. He offered his commiserations but privately he was laughing his head off. It makes our Security look totally futile. Theirs isn't."

"It is certainly a humiliation." The Weasel turned his head to Lord George. "What do you think, then – you're most directly concerned. Two of your colleagues are being held hostage, Mr Smith and his wife plus Professor Milovic, to say nothing of the Prime Minister and your niece."

Lord George had been in other Cabinets and had acquired a sense of Cabinet timing. The moment wasn't yet ripe for candour; he must let this ageing gasbag drool on. "I rather agree with that paper," he said. "The situation is entirely new and the normal procedures don't fit it at all."

161

"I can't accept that," the DPM said. "This isn't a moment for violent action."

Lord George looked round again but he could read their faces . . . *He'll persuade himself for as long as he can but sooner or later he'll have to face it. Meanwhile it's not only the French ambassador who is laughing up his well-cut sleeve.*

Lord George took a careful but measured step forwards, one towards the inevitable decision. "I see this as a question of time. The longer we let this affair drift on the longer they have to exploit us. Alternatively if we act at once we limit the damage to a matter of hours."

"What are you suggesting, please?"

"Send in the troops at once. Shoot it out."

"We can't do that," the Weasel said. He had seen the SHAME on the tabloid held up to him but it wasn't a paper he read himself. Most of the heavies had been reluctant but definite. In exceptional circumstances one must behave exceptionally. Immediate action was called for. Now. Action this day.

But not the paper he took himself. He had read the editorial twice . . . The position was grim and quite unprecedented but that would be no excuse for folly. There were new techniques of persuasion and reason; psychiatrists had proved their usefulness. The government must not be tempted into actions which could risk human lives. That wasn't the way a good liberal thought.

It was his own opinion, sincerely held, but it was a pity, he reflected now, that so very few people read his newspaper.

He could see that he was almost isolated and turned to the Lord Chancellor in hope. He was the oldest man present, an elder statesman. Moreover he was an eminent lawyer. Surely he'd be for caution; they always were. "Lord Chancellor?" he enquired and waited.

The old man lowered his massive head. It was a gesture which he had copied from Churchill. He spoke judicially as became his high office but he spoke in an abrasive demotic. "They have us by the short hairs," he said.

The DPM was disappointed for the Lord Chancellor had been putting him down. He himself had been a lecturer in a university few people had heard of. The Lord Chancellor was a fellow of the most prestigious of all the colleges. But he was a persistent man and said:

"But surely—"

"I hadn't finished."

"Please go on."

"I can see no purpose in waiting longer. If their demands are really for money and passage there'd be no reason not to say so at once. And we don't hold any Mid Eastern terrorist of a consequence to be worth a deal." He waited for a moment before he went on. The fine old head had come up to glare but now he put it down to charge. "No, I suspect they still have a card to play."

"Tell us what you're thinking."

"I am not – I haven't the evidence for serious think-ing. All I know is two facts which could point the same way. The first is that there have been no demands and the second is that they hold two women. Also for some reason there's a transmitter which we cannot suppress."

There was a shocked silence while these words were interpreted. At last the Commissioner said uncertainly: "You mean some mischief?"

"I mean a mischief going out on the air. The ultimate in humiliation."

The Weasel looked round the room a third time. He could see that he was handsomely beaten but his conscience and that leading article were insistent that he fight on while he could. And in any case these men were not humanists: they worshipped at the hated altar of a *realpolitik* which they believed solved all problems. Any dispute could be settled by force, any other standard was a trap. So now he must throw these beasts a Christian.

"So we'll alert the soldiery," – he pronounced it pejoratively – "even send them down to Wykeham on stand-by. But naturally they will take no action till my personal and express instructions. As for the rest we will follow procedure." He turned to the Commissioner of Police. "I would be grateful if you would go down to Wykeham. Talk to them yourself and report the result." He decided on another sop. "You carry more weight than a Superintendent."

"More rank, perhaps, but without your authority I do not carry an ounce more clout."

"Nevertheless I'd be glad if you'd go. If that fails we'll try the usual psychiatrist – he was successful in that affair in Belfast. Finally I will speak myself."

Somebody under his breath said: "Oh God." The Weasel couldn't tell who it was. He rose and said, a shade too quickly: "Gentlemen, that is all for today."

Lord George and the Commissioner had left the meetings side by side, walking two hundred yards before either spoke. Jack Pallant broke the silence first. "That futile Weasel. The whole thing stinks."

"It stinks to heaven. It's really frightening."

"Do you think the old man was right – the Lord Chancellor?"

"In what?"

"I meant about the women."

"He could be."

"It's never been done before."

"I would guess it's never been thought of."

"Hell."

17

Sir John Pallant, Jack to his friends, sometime private soldier in a reputable regiment, now Commissioner of Metropolitan Police and a member of the Board of the Security Executive was frustrated and in a very poor temper. He had been down to Wykeham since those were his orders and had achieved what he had expected: nothing. He shared his Superintendent's opinion that this new technique which was so much praised, the talking and the tame psychiatrist, was fallible and indeed overrated. In the present case which was clearly exceptional he thought it a total waste of time.

The two men had looked at the house from the little lodge, assessing it in their different ways. The Superintendent, a Presbyterian Scot, saw only a very comfortable sinecure for a man who had been to Oxford with the squire; but Pallant had had a much older cousin who had once held a living not so different from this one. He hadn't been a clever man and his politics would have offended the Left but he hadn't been a heretic either and he'd known every soul in his parish by name. He had also been a famous fisherman. In Pallant's private ethos he'd been worthwhile.

He asked the Superintendent now: "Have you spoken to them again?"

"No, sir. No orders to. I understood that you yourself—"

"We'll come to that later." Pallant switched his attention from the house to the grass at one side. "I don't see any bodies," he said.

"We got them back. It wasn't difficult."

"It sounds to me extremely difficult. I hope there wasn't the shooting they threatened."

The Scot said with a disciplined modesty: "As you know, sir, we're not allowed AFVs. If we were every wally in the country would scream. But we came down here in a couple of coaches and I put one in. By night, of course. It kept between the house and the bodies. They could hear it but there wasn't a moon so there wasn't much point in browning off blindly. Anyway, the coach was cover. So we picked up the bodies and brought them back in. That was easy but the driving wasn't. Backing out that coach in the dark was a tricky job. I'd like the driver commended."

"He shall be. And then?"

"Both of them were dead all right. One had been shot to shreds in the shooting but I'd guess that the other was still alive till that savage came out and finished him off. You heard the shot, of course."

"I heard the recording."

The Superintendent hesitated, then brought it out. "That's the real trouble, isn't it, sir? All this is going out on the air."

"You put it with a good policeman's restraint."

"Talking of policemen so were those two."

Pallant didn't answer him. Both were thinking the same but neither spoke. The Commissioner said at last: "I have orders and I'm going to obey them. I think they are futile and even dangerous but there they are. Where's the telephone, please?"

Jack Pallant disliked being thought a fool and was anxious to get a fool's orders behind him.

. . . Yes, it was Adam Khoury speaking.

There was an exchange of very stilted courtesies, then Pallant repeated the original question. What were the demands? How much or whom?

But that had been explained before. There were no

demands or only one. If the services were cut off it would cost a life.

And that was really all?

It was.

Pallant put the phone down, duty discharged. His orders had been to report to the Home Secretary but he had decided to go to Lord George first. Lord George was his colleague in the Security Executive and Lord George had no fancy ideas about human life.

He listened in an attentive silence but Pallant could see he was fighting anger; when he spoke it was in a voice which Sir John hadn't heard. "Go from here to the Home Secretary. Tell him what you've just told me. But I'm afraid you're not going to change his mind." He picked up a paper and passed it to Pallant. "That's the programme as the DPM sees it. There was no movement from your visit this morning so the next thing is they'll put in Amberley." Lord George answered Pallant's look of enquiry. "He's that shrink who pulled off the fluke in Ulster. But that was frightened Irish peasants and at Wykeham we're dealing with experienced terrorists. And when that fails as it certainly will the DPM will try himself."

"But that means nearly two days on the air. Forty-eight hours on our backs while they kick us. Forty-eight hours while the world laughs its head off."

"You can't change men like the DPM." Lord George grimaced. "The mining village, the slate-roofed chapel, the wicked English exploiters of the Celt. They pick up a little gloss as they rise but put them in any sort of crisis and they won't judge it by what you and I think sensible but by what fits in with their own morality."

Pallant thought a long time before answering. All his life he'd been trained to be apolitical but this was a political problem and Lord George had been a politician. "You said such men could not be changed but couldn't they be, well, superseded? At that Cabinet they were mostly against him."

167

"Several are very close to resigning. But they can't do that."

"Why not?"

"Another success for our friends at Wykeham. Think of the newspapers." Lord George swore softly. *Cabinet splits over terrorist outrage.*

"Suppose they all walked out together?"

"It's never been done – I do not know. If you're interested in the technicalities you must ask a constitutional lawyer. But it isn't going to happen in this case."

"If I may ask it again, whyever not?"

"Because there isn't a man to succeed Saint John. Without him they might not have won that election and now that they have he holds them together. There isn't another man of his stature, a man who can face a crisis and beat it. The other seniors are ragtail and bobbery, earnest liberal humanists, men convinced of their ineffable rectitude. To think that if I'd been born with money I might be something like that myself, a parlour pink or a Rolls Royce liberal."

"There's always the Lord Chancellor, though."

"The Lord Chancellor is a respected survivor. I like him and I admire him greatly. But he's knocking eighty and couldn't ride it. I don't think he would want to, either."

There was a silence while each man followed his train of thought. In fact they were the same exactly. Mention of the Lord Chancellor had lit the fuse. Jack Pallant spoke first.

"The old man was pretty Delphic, wasn't he? The two women . . . A *public* mischief . . . Do you really think – ?"

"Again I don't know. It just might be their final card of shame."

"Which woman would they choose, do you think?"

"Not Willy's wife, Amanda Smith. That would have racial overtones, make them enemies where they do not want them. If it's anyone it's going to be Sara." Lord

168

George's patrician face contorted. "I needn't tell you that she isn't my sister but we've always been rather closer than if she were." Lord George seldom raised his voice but did so now. "Damn the Home Secretary, damn him to the hell he believes in."

He recovered with an evident effort but finally managed a courteous smile. "Now be off and report to that man who isn't one. And try to keep your temper. I would not."

As Willy Smith had rightly thought the German had been carefully briefed: the rooms in the attic were much as he'd said they were. Originally two servants' bedrooms they had been turned into a flatlet for visitors with a connecting door and a bathroom in what had once been a boxroom.

The two women had been considerately treated. They'd been given an electric kettle, tea and a tin of powdered milk, and the Japanese brought them two meals a day. They weren't good meals but they kept them from hunger. They had guessed that he carried arms like the others but if he did he never showed them. On the contrary he was invariably polite for secretly he disapproved of any action which embarrassed women. It might be good terrorism but it wasn't *bushido*.

The telephone had been torn out at its socket but they'd been given an efficient radio. When the transmitter was sending they could hear only that but when it was off they could listen at pleasure. And what they heard was not reassuring. The home stations were getting impatient and angry and the foreign were quite simply contemptuous.

They had heard Jack Pallant's brief talk with Khoury and to the women upstairs it made no sense. "No demands," Amanda said. "That's unusual."

"Whatever it is they're playing it long."

"But what's the 'it'?"

"I can't be sure. But they're making us look a pack of fools."

Both women had husbands downstairs at gunpoint but they'd reached an unspoken understanding that this wasn't a subject for conversation. On that basis they were getting on admirably. Sara Saint John liked Amanda's common sense; Amanda admired Sara's evident courage. Sara said suddenly:

"Do you know Adam Khoury?"

"I'd never met him before."

"I have. In fact he tried to seduce me once."

"You've got to be joking."

"Not entirely. But 'seduce' was a pretty silly word. I went to his house intending to sleep with him. Then several things put me off and I didn't."

"You walked out on him?"

"Flat."

"He wouldn't have liked that a little bit." Amanda, to her surprise, was faintly shocked . . . A woman goes to a man, then leaves him cold. It was a scene from one of those sensitive novels she didn't read. But her common sense had been working overtime. "But they wouldn't have laid on all this just to bed you."

Sara Saint John thought carefully before she spoke. She didn't wish to alarm unnecessarily but Amanda was in this too inescapably and it wouldn't be fair if it hit her unprepared. "Not *just* to bed me," Sara said finally.

"What on earth do you mean?"

"Well, it *could* fit, couldn't it?"

"Fit into what?"

"I think I'd better dish it straight. What they're doing is to humiliate us publicly. The humiliation of enemies is immensely important to them and there is nothing they would consider more humiliating to a man than abducting his woman. If the Prime Minister's wife were raped and it went on the air . . . I'm not saying it's going to happen but if it did . . ."

Amanda had been convent educated and therefore very seldom swore. Besides, it didn't become a lady. She emitted an oath which astonished Sara, then the practical Amanda re-emerged.

"What are you going to do if it happens?"

Sara Saint John said: "I've got a gun."

"You can't have. That man felt your bag."

"He never opened it – I don't know why. And it's only a toy – the weight didn't alert him." A matter of ounces, Sara thought thankfully. A tube of cold cream and a couple of lipsticks. Nothing like a proper weapon.

"May I see it, please?" It was polite but had a ring of authority.

"You know about guns?"

"I'm not an expert. But I was in danger once, or Willy thought I was, so he gave me a gun and taught me to use it. For instance you hold it like this." She made the gesture of holding a pistol correctly. "Not what you see on the box at all. Have you ever fired this toy of yours?"

"Never." Sara fetched her bag and gave Amanda the weapon.

She looked at it in open astonishment. "I've never seen one like this in my life. Where did you get it?"

"Boyfriend in New York. Apparently you can buy them quite easily. Women carry them in their bags against muggers."

"Against whom this thing would be utterly useless." Amanda broke the weapon and looked inside. "Single shot and long .22 round. You cock the hammer and pull. No safety catch. Extremely dangerous."

"But not dangerous to the mugger?"

"If you held it against his head – "

"I'd thought of that. I thought I'd hide it under the pillow. Lying on a bed with a man – "

"Then think of something else, Mrs Sara. Suppose he ties you up first before . . . He might, you know. It's a

171

bigger indignity. So I'll keep this toy for what it's worth."
The authority had increased to command.

"What are you going to do?"

"What I can. I'll leave the connecting door ajar and if Khoury comes in I've got just one shot. I don't suppose this thing is accurate and in any case I'm not a markswoman. But I have one chance in a hundred. You have none."

Downstairs in the big living room the men had fared a lot less comfortably. They had slept in chairs or on the floor and their captors had done the same, but in pairs. Always there had been two awake and armed. By now they were dirty and heavily stubbled and silence had been an additional burden since they'd realised that any word they spoke would go out to a world agog to hear it. They hadn't been beaten or knocked about but their morale was very low indeed.

That evening the German made a gesture to Khoury who followed him into another room. "I could have called the Japanese to switch off but he's busy in the kitchen cooking. Resourceful man, that."

"That's why he was chosen."

The German lit a cigarette from a silver case. It was old and scuffed but the crest was still visible. Khoury looked at him with increasing respect. He had handled the organisation perfectly; he held a doctorate from an ancient seat; and in Germany he was a man of family. From some motive unknown he had turned to terorrism but he didn't regard this affair as a holy war. Not like that animal Palestinian who would kill and kill on his way to the *houris*. Adam Khoury had begun to fear him.

The German said: "We've been very lucky. We didn't expect the Prime Minister – only his wife. That itself is a dangerous gift from whatever gods may favour terrorism but there's an indirect advantage too. If Saint John had been outside to give orders we should probably have seen action by now but you tell me that his Deputy is notoriously indecisive and weak. He'll plan it by that new rubric of theirs, the softly-softly-catchee-monkey. Which gives us more time. Which is what we want. Yes, we have been doubly lucky."

"So what happens now?"

"By their book a psychiatrist. That will be for you, of course."

"Why not put on Milovic? *Make* him talk if he doesn't want to."

"What would be the point of that?"

"He's an Ishmael in the world of psychologists. He looks in rather worse shape than the others. Finally he's a quick-tempered man."

"You think they might quarrel?"

"There's a very good chance of it."

"Excellent," the German said. "I'd never have thought of that myself. The Pasha was clever to send you. I'm glad you came."

Khoury could see that his rating had risen. It would be in order to ask another question. "And after that?"

"Another delay for another meeting. Clement Saint John would not have done that. Then, if the luck is with us still, we'll get the DPM in person. From what you tell me that's a near certainty. He's the sort who would feel it a private duty even though he'll be advised to the contrary."

"The last move in their book before they send in the soldiers. I'm surprised they're not on station already."

"They are," the German said.

"I didn't hear them."

"Nor did I. But I've been upstairs and had a look." There was a faint hint of reproof but it was delivered courteously. "The main body is in that meadow oppo-site, where the coach park was when they were running the fête, and there's a detachment in what's left of the funfair."

"When do you think they'll send them in?"

"Sometime after you've snubbed the DPM. And the timing is going to be very important. The soldiers may be their last ploy. It isn't ours."

"I know," Adam Khoury said. "I know."

The German gave him a curious glance. Partly it was one of doubt but mixed with it was a certain sympathy. For reasons which he preferred not to think of he had changed his comfortable life to an outlaw's but some of the old taboos had followed him. If ordered to do what Khoury must he would have done it and then shot himself in disgust. He wouldn't read Adam Khoury easily. He seemed to be a gentleman but he was going to do something which shamed his class. The German said a little tentatively:

"I gather you gave your word to the Pasha."

Adam Khoury said: "I did."

So that was it: he had given his word and was therefore bound by it. The German could understand that and said:

"In which case a word of most friendly warning. Cut down on the drinking, and quite a bit."

Adam Khoury had found a case of brandy. It was good brandy and he'd been drinking it freely.

"I'm used to brandy."

"I know you are. I've nothing against an occasional drink – I drink myself when I'm not on duty. But alcohol is a tricky drug." It was one man of the world advising another. "Up to a point it increases desire. Beyond it it induces impotence. And that wouldn't do at all, now would it?"

Khoury had turned to go back to the living room but the German put a hand on his shoulder. "One other thing since we're speaking in friendship. Watch that bloody Arab carefully. He hates you."

"You've felt that too? But he also loathes you."

"I know he does." The German gave a shrug of

174

dismissal. "He hates me as part of the class war he's been cloned with but I'm also a colleague whom he can trust. I've a solid reputation behind me. You have none and he doesn't trust you an inch."

They returned to the living room and a very small brandy. Khoury was remembering what the Pasha had told him, that he would accept revenge as an adequate motive. So it had seemed at the time to Khoury too. Now he was conscious the flame was cooling and alcohol was an unreliable surrogate.

18

Of the three men held downstairs in the living room Milo was showing the strain the most obviously. In his boyhood in his own troubled country his family had been arrested and held, and though they had been later released the experience had left a mental wound. Moreover he had a fastidious stomach and tinned and frozen food didn't suit it. He liked plenty of roughage, as much fruit as he could lay hands on, and his bowels hadn't opened for forty hours. He suspected that they weren't going to this morning and the penalty for regular bowels was feeling disproportionately off colour when they failed. Finally his professional interest was the vagaries of the human animal and his knowledge warned him, rather louder than the others, that something very unusual was in the air. He was in a very bad temper that Saturday morning when the telephone rang again for the third time.

The German answered it but turned to Khoury. "Have you ever heard of a man called Amberley?"

Adam Khoury shook his head.

"But I have." It had been Milo speaking. "He's a fraud, a conman. He's a consultant in some misguided hospital but he's madder than the patients he treats."

"He announced himself as Sir Harry."

"He would. He got a knighthood for that affair in Ulster which was going to collapse within hours in any case. Now he's some sort of official mandarin."

"I'd like you to take his call just the same."

"I'd very much rather not. He and his sort make me sick. We haven't an idea in common."

"Nevertheless I prefer that you speak with him."
There'd been no movement of the German's weapon, no melodrama, no overt threat. The voice had been enough and Milo rose. He moved a little shakily but it was from stiffness rather than evident fear.

"Milovich here."

"Why Milo!" Milo considered this an impertinence. He wasn't on short-name terms with Sir Henry.

"What can I do for you?"

"Tell me what's happening."

"I can tell you what you'll already know. There are three of us here in the room downstairs and two women in the bedrooms above us. Of the four men holding us—"

Milo gave the German a quick look of enquiry but the German nodded and said: "Go on." He had nothing to fear from a recital of detail.

"Of the four men holding us one is a well-spoken German. The second seems to be some sort of Arab. There is also a man called Adam Khoury and a Japanese with a Field Service transmitter. I'm inclined to think it's quite a powerful one."

"I didn't mean your dispositions."

"Then what did you mean?"

"I meant the, well, the atmosphere."

"The atmosphere is a little stuffy."

"You're not being very helpful."

"I can't be. We simply haven't a language in common."

There was a long silence before Amberley spoke again. "Are you speaking under duress?"

"Not so far. But you'll realise all this is going out on the air."

Amberley said stiffly: "I have my instructions."

"Bloody silly ones."

There was another and even longer silence before Amberley spoke again. "What's the state of your captors?"

177

"They appear in good health."

"I meant psychologically."

Milo looked at the German again who this time shook his head. The Palestinian was some way from cracking but a child could see that the waiting had taken its toll. He was itching for the killings which fed him.

Milo said carefully: "You can say that there is a certain tension."

"Anyone in particular?"

"Me for one."

"Is that all?"

"I'm afraid it is. Except that if you've the means to do so you could send me in some syrup of figs."

The German took the telephone, returning it to its cradle decisively. "You did that very well," he said. He turned to the others and spoke to them generally. "And that concludes the entertainment, I suspect until tomorrow morning." He might have been a first-class umpire drawing stumps at a Festival match between good club sides.

The two women had been listening upstairs. Both had been puzzled and Amanda spoke first.

"I don't think that helped much."

"I expect he had a gun in his back."

"He didn't sound frightened, he sounded bad tempered."

"Amberley is a fashionable psychiatrist. The conventional sort which Milo despises. Anyway, they got nothing from him."

"Except," Amanda said, "except time." She walked to the bedroom window and looked out. "The soldiers have put up tents but I don't see a man. No drilling or marching about at all."

"They're not that sort of soldier, you know."

"When do you think they'll come in?"

"If Clement had still been in charge they'd be in by now."

"The longer this goes on—"

"I know."

"And you still really think . . . What you said before?"

"It's the sort of thing an Arab terrorist would think of, the final gesture of the contempt he felt for us. But if it happens I won't give a trick away. No crying or pleading." She contrived a smile but it wasn't a happy one. "Not even a grunt."

"I suppose he could give a running commentary."

"I doubt if he'll do that. Unconvincing. So there you are, or rather I am. I've never been raped before. I wonder—"

Amanda said: "I still have the pistol."

"Which you put at a hundred to one."

"I did. But I'm thinking that was optimistic."

Downstairs the German was counting his blessings and these included Adam Khoury. It had been a brilliant idea of the Pasha's to send him too. He had dealt with two calls from the police unexceptionably, insisting there were no demands nor any price, keeping them uneasily up in the air; and his idea of putting on Milo to answer Amberley had been shrewd in principle and effective in practice.

Moreover he'd given essential advice. The German had been well informed about the character of Clement Saint John, how he would react and how quickly when the news was brought to Downing Street that his wife was being held at Wykeham. But as it had happened he wasn't at Downing Street; he was here at Wykeham, captive with his wife. An enormous piece of uncovenanted luck but at the same time with a disadvantage. For the German had been given no briefing on the man who would act in the Prime Minister's absence.

But Khoury had informed him confidently. He had met him and his opinion was low. He was a man of an endangered species, the solid as rock non-comformist Liberal, the antithesis of Clement Saint John.

179

Translated into practical terms that meant that there would be more delay. Amberley would return to London with nothing to show but an ill-tempered snubbing. There'd be another indecisive meeting with maybe a second opinion to muddle it and then the Home Secretary would demand to sleep on it. Unnecessary violence must be avoided at any price. But he'd come to Wykeham himself in the end: Khoury had been convinced of that. It would be a matter of duty, of private conscience, and in the Weasel that organ was highly developed.

So there'd be no further action till tomorrow at earliest. For the hostages that was three nights on the rack. The German looked at all three in turn. They'd been spoken to with a cold correctness; they'd been fed and allowed to relieve their needs. But their conditions had been made uncomfortable and none of them, except Willy some time ago, was used to any sustained discomfort. Milo had shown that he'd taken it worst. He was edgy and irritable and occasionally he grimaced to suppress a tic. Willy sat stolidly when he wasn't sleeping (he slept on the floor, the others in chairs) but his handsome face was drawn and anxious. Only the Prime Minister seemed unaffected. He was growing a very promising beard and he'd been the first to realise that speech played into his captors' hands. Except for an occasional "Thank you," when the Japanese brought him food on a tray he hadn't said a word to anyone. He sat silently, tightly controlled, his own man.

The German looked round the room again, nodding. They had really been extraordinarily lucky. All four were living on borrowed time. When the soldiers did come in they'd have no chance. For himself he was sincerely indifferent; he had nothing to live for, he'd burnt his boats. The Japanese? He would die with dignity. Death was another sacrament, no more. The Palestinian would be well content provided he took an enemy with him.

Only Adam Khoury was worrying. Up to a point he'd been an unmixed asset but beyond that point lay a very real doubt. For the German had sensed what the Pasha had known, that the consuming fire of insensate terrorism was unlit in this westernised Arab's belly. But he was still the essential, the irreplaceable actor in the final scene of this obscene little drama.

But the German looked at him with disapproval. It was barely eleven o'clock in the morning but already Khoury had drunk quite a lot. He wasn't drunk but he wasn't sober. If he went on like this for the rest of the day, perhaps for part of the night as well . . .

He would have to be formally, finally warned. He signalled him outside the room again.

The German hesitated. The instincts which he had carried over from a life before the fever had caught him forbad that he humiliate a man whom he considered a gentleman before another who was clearly not. He made up his mind and asked politely:

"Can you speak German?"

"Not colloquially."

"Then French?"

"Of course."

The German's French was correct but stilted. "I tried to warn you as a colleague. Now I must go further than that. I'm still in charge of what isn't political and getting drunk is not a political act. It isn't even a wise one – it's madness. A drunken man cannot do what you must."

What you promised to do, the German was thinking. He wouldn't have given that promise himself, he couldn't even understand how a man could conceivably give it, but then he wasn't a Christian Arab.

"I told you before, I can handle brandy."

19

The Weasel had risen at six o'clock, something he found quite easy to do since he liked to be in bed by ten. His conscience was clear, he was doing his duty and, fortified by these pious emotions, he ate a breakfast rather larger than usual. Normally he had to eat carefully for he was putting on weight and it didn't suit him.

He enjoyed the drive to Wykeham greatly. Unlike the Prime Minister he relished attention, the armed man beside him, the cars in front and behind with more policemen. The convoy was driven fast and well and by half past ten had arrived at Wykeham. The Home Secretary got out at the lodge and went inside. The police had been warned of his coming and were correct – no more. He wasn't on happy terms with the police for under pressure from his vocal Left he had let them down badly more than once. The Superintendent, now in uniform, saluted. "Good morning, sir." He held out the telephone.

In the living room all seven men heard it ring. The German nodded at Khoury who took it.

"The Home Secretary here." The voice came through on the speaker clearly and clearer to the world outside the room.

"My name is Khoury. I will take any message."

"I want to speak to the Prime Minister. Personally."

"I'm afraid that will be quite impossible."

"I have a right," the offended voice said. "I insist."

"Insist away by all means. It amuses us."

Adam Khoury was conscious of a movement behind him. The Prime Minister had unexpectedly risen. He was stiff from sitting but moved fast and decisively. He snatched the telephone from Khoury, said:

"Send in the soldiers at once. That's an order."

The Arab raised his gun and fired once. He shot Clement Saint John but not to kill.

The Prime Minister fell backwards into a chair. He realised he hadn't been mortally wounded but there was a bullet in his left shoulder just the same. It wasn't yet hurting much but that would come.

The women upstairs had heard the shot on the radio. They looked at each other but neither spoke. Finally Sara said:

"Give me that gun back."

"Utter madness."

"Give it me, woman."

"For Christ's sake be quiet."

The German said to the Arab coldly: "You shouldn't have done that."

"Why not?"

"Because it cuts our time to the bone. The order to send the soldiers in is something which they might just have ignored but they'll have heard that shot and that will decide it. I give us ten minutes at most for the final scene."

He looked down at Adam Khoury, slumped in a chair, his expression half of pity, half of contempt. For Khoury had ignored his warning and was now blind drunk beyond hope of venery. The German hadn't attempted to stop him by force. For one thing he had some sympathy which he tried to suppress; and for another he had worked it out that completion of the act wasn't vital. The woman would protest and weep and that would go out on the air as planned. This was radio, not television. So long as Khoury could stand and speak he could play his disgraceful part to some purpose. The German turned to the Japanese.

183

"Nip upstairs and wire up. And be quick about it. We haven't any time to lose."

The Japanese knocked on the door before unlocking it. He had always done that, it was only polite, but this morning his face wasn't smiling but set. He said to Sara: "Good morning, madam. Where is the other lady, please?"

"In her bedroom, lying down. We heard the shot."

"I see."

It was none of his business and he was thankful it wasn't. His orders had been to wire up. He did so. He had brought the transmitter and with it the microphone. The loudspeaker wasn't necessary so he had left it in the drawing room. He plugged them in and tested both. Then he went into the landing and squatted down.

He was a decent and therefore unhappy man, but at least he hadn't been ordered to watch an act which he considered barbarous. The ways of the mysterious West had never ceased to puzzle and shock him. All he knew was that he was going to die and that his ancestors wouldn't welcome him honourably.

Downstairs the German said: "All yours."

Adam Khoury poured another brandy. The German said: "No," but he spoke too late. Finally Adam Khoury rose. He felt his way out of the room and up the stairs. The squatting Japanese ignored him.

The Japanese had left the door open. Sara whispered to Amanda Smith: "There's somebody coming up the stairs."

"I heard him too."

"Don't shoot before you must."

"I won't."

Khoury came in and looked round foolishly. He seemed to be having trouble focussing. He didn't inquire for Amanda Smith. Both women could see he was helplessly drunk.

184

He walked to the bed and stopped there uncertainly. Sara hadn't moved from the chair.

"Get on the bed." It was barely intelligible.

Sara didn't answer him.

Astonishingly he said: "Please. Please."

He'd been holding on to the bedhead for support. Now he slipped to the floor in slow motion. He stayed there for perhaps ten seconds and the women could hear him breathing with difficulty. Then he pulled himself up by the bed and swayed dangerously. Finally, using the walls, he reached the door. They heard him faltering down the stairs . . . Slowly, very slowly, despairingly . . .

He reached the drawing room and all five men stared at him. None of them spoke but all of them knew.

The Arab cut him in two with a lingering burst.

There was a long silence till the German spoke again. "You bloody fool. You've wrecked the whole plan."

"He was useless, a traitor. He's better dead." The Palestinian spat. "Now I'll have to do the job myself and this time it's going to get finished properly."

Sara Saint John he ignored without greeting, walking straight into Amanda's bedroom. She was lying on the bed, a sheet over her. He pulled it down and looked at her thoughtfully. She had buried her face in the pillow like a child and she didn't have to act to be trembling.

"Stay where you are and you won't get hurt."

He went back into the other room. Sara Saint John was still in her chair.

"Take your clothes off and get on the bed."

She didn't move.

He made a gesture with his gun and said: "I shan't kill you but I shall wound you painfully."

Sara rose and began to undress deliberately. The Arab said unexpectedly: "Stop. The rest will be my personal pleasure. Get on the bed."

Sara Saint John lay down on it silently, fighting to

185

breathe regularly and above all things not to look at the other door. Behind it was Amanda Smith with a pistol and maybe a chance in a hundred.

The Arab had stripped to the waist by now and she could see that he was distastefully hairy. The resentments of centuries were discharged in a single word.

Sara stayed silent and he said it again.

Don't look at that door. If you do it's finished.

A hand had begun to move lower when it stopped. There was a faint but clear report and he staggered. He put his hand to his head in a gesture of disbelief. Then he fell in an untidy heap.

Downstairs there was a much louder explosion. More accurately there were two explosions since they'd thrown one in from each end of the room. Stun grenades weren't designed to make smoke but one of them had blown out the fireplace and the room was full of a fog of ash. The fire had not been lighted yet but there'd been logs on a six-inch bed of cinders.

Willy had gone down at once, by the fireplace where the smoke was thickest. He was shocked and thinking with a total inconsequence . . . They'd have to change the rule book a bit. Don't use stun grenades in country houses which as often as not have open grates . . .

The German had gone down too but got up again. His weapon was still on its sling round his neck but his arms were at his sides, at attention. This wasn't the way a gentleman died, not brawling it out with automatics, not behaving like a Twenties gangster. As the smoke thinned a soldier saw him and shot him dead. He did it with a single shot for these were highly trained men who knew their business. You didn't fire bursts into rooms with hostages.

The smoke had almost cleared by now and the leading soldier looked down at the floor. "That's two," he said, "but two to go." He turned to Clement Saint John. He was still in his chair.

186

"The Prime Minister?"

"I have that honour." His left arm was hanging loose at his side and blood had begun to stain his jacket. "The other two are upstairs with the women. One is a Japanese with his box, the other is an Arab with a gun."

The soldier saluted. "We'll go and collect them." He made a signal to another man. "You come with me and make it sharpish."

Upstairs they had heard the stun grenades, then a single shot and now boots on the stairs. On the boards of the passage the boots sounded different. There were two single shots as the Japanese fired and the boots ran back to the staircase and cover. Then the unmistakable crack of a real grenade. The firing stopped.

Two men came into the room, one limping. Both wore black masks and no badges of rank but the unwounded one was clearly an officer.

"Are you all right?"

"We're both in one piece." Sara had got most of her clothes back.

The officer walked to the dead Arab by the bed; he was lying face down and he turned him over. "Nasty little hole in the head." Amanda had dropped the gun on the floor and the limping soldier picked it up. He broke it and looked inside; he whistled.

"I've never seen a thing like this."

"American," Sara said. "For muggings."

The officer took the gun from the soldier. Held against a man's head it would kill but also it would leave a powderburn and the Arab's face hadn't shown the least sign of one. He thought carefully before he spoke again. What was said or done now was going to be vital. Finally he asked deliberately:

"Which of you ladies is 'Annie Get Your Gun'?"

"I am," Sara said. "The pistol's mine."

20

The Prime Minister was still in hospital, Willy Smith was discreetly hiding from the press and Milo was up to his neck in a lawsuit. So the Security Executive was in no sort of shape for formal meetings. But Lord George and Jack Pallant had been lunching quietly, each man in very expert control of the aspect of the affair which concerned him. Over coffee Lord George was saying contentedly:

"So the Prime Minister is a national hero and we haven't had that since the Duke of Wellington. A good deal of damaging stuff went out but the end was a handsome win to us." He waved a hand. "Prime Minister with a gun behind him gives orders to send in the soldiers at once when he knows that what his captors want is further time to make us look silly. Prime Minister is duly shot but when the soldiers come in gives them clear instructions. People are lapping it up by the gallon."

"Will he call a snap election?"

"Certainly not. If there's one thing my nephew by marriage is it's decent and almost painfully honest. Moreover he has no need to do so. There are four by-elections up in the air and the pollsters say he'll win at least three of them. Further, he's got what he privately wanted, or more correctly he's got a large part of it. As you know, what he really wanted was a diplomat on open trial before a British court. He can't have that since Khoury is dead and in any case he was no longer a diplomat. But he was an ex-Ambassador to the Court of St James's who was engaged in an overt act of terrorism,

188

one of a peculiarly unpleasant kind. In my poor opinion that's enough, or at least for several years it's enough. Our plumed and brocaded friends will walk warily. By any count that's a national advantage as well as a feather in the Prime Minister's personal cap." Lord George looked at Jack Pallant hard. "And your side?" he asked.

"It was fortunate Sara Saint John kept her head. There'll have to be an inquest of course, but there's only one conceivable verdict." Pallant waved a hand in turn but less largely. "Woman about to be raped by stranger. So shoots him dead to loud applause. Sara is a heroine too, particularly in the lesser papers. Of course she shouldn't have had an unlicensed gun and probably she'll be fined for that. Who cares? She defended the honour of British womanhood or so I read in the women's pages."

"But that gun – ?"

"The fingerprints, you mean? All in order: it had just about everybody's. There were Amanda's and the two soldiers who picked it up. Happily also Sara's quite clearly. Of course the forensic boys could tear it to pieces: the angle of entry was wrong for one thing." An eyelid dropped and rose again smoothly. "But no forensic wizard will have motive to pry. I'll see to that."

"I'm sure you will. Have a brandy. In passing, it was Khoury's drink."

"The more pleasure in downing it."

Amanda and Willy Smith were smoking a small one. They took four drags each in turn, then threw it away. Willy said:

"That was marvellous shooting."

"You taught me."

"I had you taught. In a limited and discreet little circle you're a heroine, Grade A with knobs on, but I'm afraid you're not going to get a gong. For one thing the Executive doesn't deal in them and for another the accepted story is that Sara did the shooting, not you."

"I don't want a silly gong."

"I'm sure. What you've got is a month's holiday, all paid. Officially they had to award it to me but they made it clear it was you who earned it."

"Very handsome of them."

"Yes. They may not issue gongs or citations but they can and they do reward good service. Now where would you like to go?"

"To Brighton," she said at once.

Willy laughed. His wife had a fixation on Brighton and one which he understood very well. Before they'd been married or even engaged she had carried him off and there seduced him. And their second son had started life in that city.

"Not Brighton, I'm afraid, my dear. One of the terms of this little arrangement is that we go somewhere abroad and there lie low. They're not frightened I'll boob like Milo did, they just want to protect us from hordes of journalists."

"Then somewhere warm."

"The West Indies, for instance?"

She shook her head. "Not there. I haven't the least desire to go back. Here we do pretty well – we're accepted. But you know what would happen there? I'll tell you. Such Whites as are left would stare at our clothes, ask us where we learnt our English, and the Blacks would think we were Uncle Toms."

"Lord George suggested Cyprus, then. Turkish Cyprus, of course. The Greeks have turned the rest into a Mediterranean Blackpool. Anyway, I mistrust them. And Lord George has it buttoned up very neatly. He has a contact there who owes us a favour and Turks can be pretty firm with journalists."

"What's the weather like now?"

"You can swim in the sea still. And if you can stomach the food it's a breathtaking country."

190

"I can stomach the food if I have to."

"Done."

Sara was visiting her husband in hospital. He was sitting up in bed but he hadn't shaved. "And how's the national hero this morning?"

"Comfortable. The bullet's out and I'm not in pain. And talking of heroes you're a bigger."

"My heroism was thinking fast."

"You certainly did that. I'm proud."

"And yours was physical courage. I'm prouder."

She gave him a look which he hadn't seen for some years. "Have you heard about Milo?"

"Only the outlines. He gave an interview to a newspaper, which as an official he should never have done."

"He gave it for a great deal of money. I don't approve of men who do that."

"And in it he libelled that psychiatrist Amberley. By his lights he was telling the truth, the whole truth, but what he said was an inexcusable libel."

"He doesn't like men like Sir Henry Amberley."

"I'm afraid that won't impress a court."

"What I don't understand is why the newspaper passed it. Surely they've lawyers who read for libel?"

The Prime Minister shrugged and wished he hadn't. The gesture had brought a sharp spasm of pain; he gasped.

"For Christ's sake be careful, Clem." Like that very female look the 'Clem'. was new.

He noticed it but answered her question. "I would guess the newspaper balanced the odds. On the one hand probably swingeing damages and on the other an increased circulation. Which I gather is dramatically happening."

"But Milo is in it too?"

"Unavoidably."

"He didn't behave impeccably. You did."

191

"I was running scared," he said.

"Any fool can be brave when he isn't frightened. But going back to Milo's libel, will he lose his job on the Security Executive?"

"Not if I can help it – no. He may have an outsize chip on his shoulder but he's much too valuable to lose for nothing."

"Nothing?"

"Let's call it an indiscretion, then."

"You're a very loyal man. I like that too. I also like your beard. Beards *send* me."

"I'll shave as soon as I can do it comfortably."

"Please don't. An imperial, I rather thought. Little tuft on the chin and a spike underneath. Van Dyke portrait and there you are."

"Where's that?"

Sara didn't answer directly. "How long do you think it will take?"

"Say three weeks."

"Three whole weeks? I can't wait that long."